I FELL IN LOVE
WITH A
REAL STREET
THUG

3

THE FINALE

A NOVEL BY

PEBBLES STARR

www.jadedpublications.com

CH

TO BE NOTIFIED OF NEW RELEASES,
CONTESTS, GIVEAWAYS,

AND BOOK SIGNINGS IN YOUR AREA, TEXT
BOOKS TO **25827**

PROLOGUE

TINO

Laying up in a hospital bed was not at all how I imagined the morning after my grand opening. As I looked down at the cast on my hand, I felt like a mothafucking fool. I'd made myself an easy lick by promoting the club so heavily. If there was anyone to blame for the shit that went down, it was me.

After Kylie was released, I didn't hear from her again. And when I tried to hit her up a few hours ago, the call went straight to voicemail. I didn't want to believe that she'd blocked a nigga out of spite, but maybe this street shit was just too much for her. At the end of the day, I couldn't blame her for taking a step back. The dangerous lifestyle that I lived wasn't meant for a full-time live in girlfriend. And perhaps her life just wasn't meant for a savage nigga like me.

All of a sudden, Touché entered the room, snapping me out of my thoughts. The last time I saw him he was going after Shane and his crew. "Aye, wus good, bruh? You end up handling that?"

Touché chuckled and took a seat next to my bed. "Nah, nigga. Them mothafuckas was gone long before I even started the engine. But don't worry. Them pussies gon' be dealt with sooner or later. I got eyes and ears on the streets."

I wouldn't rest until those mothafuckas

were dead "That's what's up. But you came all the way here to tell me that?"

Touché scratched behind his ear. "Nah, bruh...I actually came to handle something else."

Before I could ask what he meant, Touché pulled out a handgun with a suppressor screwed on the end. Pointing it in my direction, he rested his index finger on the trigger. At any moment, I expected him to squeeze, and the anticipation alone killed me.

"How much Cue paying you?" Touché asked. "And ain't no need to bullshit. I already put two and two together. Yo' ass was stalling for a reason. You wasn't ever gon' body that nigga 'cuz you playin' for his team. So tell me...how much did it take for you to switch up?"

Licking my dry lips, I swallowed the large lump in throat. "Twice as much as Aubrey paid us."

Touché chuckled. "That's funny as fuck," he said. "The nigga Aubrey paid me three times as much to kill you."

Damn.

They say greed, in the end, fails even the greedy.

If I had just done what we were supposed to do, I would never be in this situation.

"C'mon now, man. We brothers—"

"Nah, we ain't mothafucking brothers. You wasn't 'bout to split that money with me. You out for self...and I ain't mad at that, nigga, 'cuz so am I. That's just how the game go," Touché said. "And you should know how grimy this game can be."

PFEW!

Suddenly, and without warning, Touché shot me in the chest at point blank range.

My eyes shot in open in surprise before a sharp pain tore through my body. Never in a million years did I see this shit coming.

"You should've stuck to the mothafucking plan, G. It might've just saved ya life."

Touché lifted his gun to my head. There was no sympathy in his eyes as he prepared to take my life. No regret, no pity. It was like we were never boys. Like we didn't grow up and get money together.

That dollar can make a mothafucka switch lanes quick.

The last thing I heard was a gunshot before everything went black.

KHARI

That morning, I stopped by Mama's house to check on her and Kylie. I'd saw the news and heard about what happened at the club, and I knew the family wanted to be together after losing Starr. We may've had our differences, but she was still family at the end of the day.

When I got to Mama's house, there were a few people already in attendance. She and Kylie had prepared a dinner for our closest relatives in order to celebrate the life of Starr. There was also a memorial on the mantle in the living room, which displayed all of her old photos. All of the pictures were taken before she started hanging in the streets and falling in with the wrong crowd.

I felt so sorry for Starr. She didn't deserve to be brutally killed, and I wouldn't have wished her death on my worst enemy.

After getting the news about Starr's murder, Cue caught the first thing back to Atlanta. As always, he was there to help out and support us doing our time of need. He even insisted on taking care of the funeral arrangements but I told him that we'd cover it. Besides, he had already done enough for our family.

To be honest, I couldn't quite tell how Starr's death had affected him. Cue didn't seem as distraught as I thought he'd be, and I found that somewhat odd, considering the length of time they'd been together.

I thought about addressing it but figured it wasn't appropriate because of the circumstances. Plus, it really wasn't my business how he chose to cope with the loss of his ex.

After helping Mama cook and clean, we exchanged old stories about Starr and all of the good times we shared growing up together. By the time the sun went down, everyone started slowly dispersing. Cue and I decided to hang back until all of the guests were gone. I wanted to talk to Kylie in private before I left.

She was in her old room when I knocked on her door and waited for her to invite me in.

"Who is it?" she called out.

"Khari."

"Come on in, sis."

Kylie had just stepped into a pair of pajama pants when I walked in. There was a nasty bruise on her head but I refrained from asking how she'd gotten it. I figured if she wanted to talk about it she'd tell me.

"Wassup?"

I took a seat on the edge of her bed. She still had all of her childhood posters plastered all over the walls. *Will this girl ever grow up*, I wondered.

I then remembered who I was talking about. *I strongly doubt it.*

"Is there anything you wanna talk about? Everything alright?"

There was a long pause before she answered.

"You know what, Khari? I'd love to be able to confide in you...but I don't have any energy to listen to you tell me you told me so. I know that I have dodgy taste in men. I know that I make a lot of the same stupid mistakes. And one day...I'mma learn. But it's something I gotta do on my own. So to answer your question, no...I don't wanna talk. But thanks for the invite."

"Okay," I said, standing to my feet. I wouldn't dare argue with her. "The offer's there if ever you change your mind, sis."

"Thanks," she smiled.

"I love you."

"I love you too."

Walking out of her bedroom, I closed the door behind me. Kylie wanted a break from the thugs and all that street shit, and I couldn't have agreed more. Some time for herself would do her some good, because if she didn't slow down, she'd be headed down the same deadly path as Starr.

After making sure that Mama was okay, me and Ali left with Cue and headed back home. When we pulled into the driveway, he switched the gears to park and sat there for a moment. Ali had already fallen asleep in the back seat.

"I know you had a long day...but I think I should come inside so we can talk."

Cue was right. There was nothing I wanted more than a hot shower and to lay my head on the pillow. But he seemed intent on saying whatever was on his mind so I agreed. "Okay...Let me get Ali out the backseat—"

"Don't worry about it," he said. "I got 'em."

Turning off the engine, he climbed out the car and opened the back door. Carefully lifting Ali in his arms, he carried him to the front of the house. After opening the door, Cue took him to his room and gently laid him in his bed.

I removed Ali's shoes and Cue pulled the comforter over him. Afterwards, I kissed my son on the forehead and left out of his room with Cue. "What's up? What did you have to talk to me about?"

"There's been a lot of shit going on lately," he said. "And I don't think I feel safe with you and Ali staying here anymore."

I laughed because I thought he was joking at first. "Are you serious?"

"I think a fresh start can be good for you and Ali—"

"Stop talking like you know what's best for me and my son!" I snapped. "He's been living in this house all his life. Who the hell do you think you are to come along and uproot him?"

Cue's jaw muscle tightened. "You know damn well who I am to him, Khari. You've known all this time."

Tears filled my eyes as I stared at him in utter silence.

"You looked me in the face and told me he was Aubrey's...but he isn't. And you've known that for over seven years," he said. "How could you keep something like that from me? From him?"

A single tear rolled down my cheek. "How did you...?"

"I had him tested while he was in the hospital."

My mouth fell open in shock. I couldn't believe what the hell I was hearing. I trusted him to be around my son and he pulled some shit like that? "What?! You swabbed my son's mouth behind my fucking back?! Is that what the fuck you're telling me?"

Cue was silent.

"Who the fuck do you think you are to do some shit like that? And while he was laying up in the fucking hospital! What the fuck is wrong with you, Cue? What the fuck is wrong with you?"

"No, what the fuck is wrong with you? Letting me believe he was some other man's child. What type of woman does some shit like that?"

"You had no right to do that shit, Cue! You had no mothafucking right!"

"You had no right to lie to me."

Honestly, I'd been lying to myself for so long about Ali that I had started believing it. Even though I knew what I was doing was wrong, I still went with it. I allowed Aubrey to think that Ali was his out of fear of what my friends and family would think about me.

Cue and Starr were still together when we slipped up and had sex with each other. I didn't want to complicate things between them or my cousin, so I lied. And when Cue moved away, he made it even easier to keep up the lie. Besides, I didn't want my son growing up without a father. When Aubrey came around the timing was perfect so I pinned the pregnancy on him.

"You had no right," I continued to cry. I couldn't think of shit else to say since I knew I was wrong.

Cue walked up and pulled me towards him, enveloping me in a cloud of his Invictus cologne. He kissed my tears away and made me feel like everything was going to be okay.

Lifting me in his strong muscled arms, he carried me to the bedroom. Once inside, he gently placed me on the mattress and eased out of his clothes. Afterwards, he slowly undressed me and slipped between my thighs.

"*Unh.*"

We groaned in unison as he pushed himself inside my tight, wet walls. Cue pinned my legs so far back that my toes touched the headboard. "Yeah...that's it. Open up. Lemme get deep in this shit." He brought my foot towards his mouth and started sucking on my toes. That shit drove me crazy every time.

"Oh my goodness, Cue. Oh my goodness." I was breathing hard and heavy as he stroked my spot at a slow and steady pace. "You feel so good baby."

Cue nodded his head arrogantly. "Yeah, this where I need to be," he said. His strokes were circular and deep, and powerful. "This where I should've been all along. Right here with you...every single day..."

"*Every single day?*" I asked.

Cue went deeper. "Every single fucking day," he said before kissing me.

"I love you, Constantine."

"I love you too, baby."

Cue flipped me over so that I was on my stomach and entered me swiftly from behind. Interlocking our fingers, he fucked me passionately and intensely. Cue was quite the romantic lover.

"Damn, you're about to make cum!" I bellowed.

"Cum on yo' dick, baby," he coached. "Cum all over it." He slipped his finger inside my mouth to suck on while I came all over his dick. "Yeah...that's it...Cum for me, baby..."

I shivered in delight. No one could satisfy me the way he did.

I was so close to cumming a second time when I heard the sound of the front door being kicked open. My initial thought was that someone was running up in my crib to rob us. Instead, a gang of DEA agents stormed inside the bedroom with their guns drawn.

"Constantine Saldana, you're under arrest."

Before I could figure out what was going on, he was handcuffed.

"What the fuck is this about?"

"You have the right to remain silent. Anything you say can and will be used against you in a court of law."

"Cue?! What's happening?"

"You have the right to consult an attorney. If you cannot afford an attorney, one will be appointed for you. Do you understand?"

"Cue, say something!" I called after him.

"I understand," he said, ignoring me.

In tears, I watched as he was escorted out of the house in nothing but a pair of jeans. Everyone in the neighborhood was standing outside of their homes watching.

With the sheet wrapped tightly around my body, I followed them outside where they had the whole block lit up with police cruisers.

"Cue?!" My voice cracked with emotion as I waited for an explanation. Hell, for anything. "Cue, talk to me! What's going on?"

"I'm sorry, Khari," he said before they placed him in the backseat.

Sadly, I had lost another man that I loved to the system.

I FELL IN LOVE WITH A

REAL STREET NIGGA

3

THE FINALE

1

AUBREY

I should've known you would cross me...

I should've known you would cross me...

Lil' Wayne and Future's collabo track poured through the speakers of the Beats pill as I snorted a coke line off the kitchen table in victory. You would've thought a nigga was off papers based on the amount of drugs I consumed.

Shit. Fuck the consequences.

This win was worth celebrating. After taking the rap for a nigga that turned around and smashed my baby moms, it felt good to have a lil' retribution. Hell, I deserved it. No one was more loyal to him than me and fucking Khari was how he'd decided to repay me.

The day Cue looked me in the eye and told me he'd raise my son, I knew that I couldn't let up on his ass. The fuck nigga had to go. Plug or no plug. At this point, it wasn't even 'bout the connect or the mothafucking money. It was about respect—something that nigga Cue obviously lacked. And coming up, I was always taught that disrespect was the weapon of the weak, and the streets ain't have no room for the weak.

Neither did Khari.

She was rocking with that nigga now, but

she would forever be mine—even after death. And the only way a nigga could ever take my bitch from me was by prying her from my cold, dead fingers. I'd never let her go without a fight.

That pussy belonged to me.

Hell, just the thought of being inside them wet, tight walls made me harder than a mothafucka. Khari had that shit a nigga would kill for—or go to extreme lengths to protect.

A smiled a little when I thought about the stupid ass look that was probably on Cue's face after the police stormed in. He had no idea that I had struck a deal with the law to bring down his drug empire.

There was only room for one at the top.

Damn. A nigga had only been free a couple of days, but I was making a year's worth of moves. Cue was in custody, Tino was on his way to the mortuary. I was on a mothafucking roll.

The sudden sound of the front door opening interrupted my thoughts. I smelled her Chanel perfume before she even entered the room. A few seconds later, my baby mama Leah appeared in the doorway of the kitchen. She was holding a few shopping bags and rocking a pair of oversized sunglasses. The bitch looked like a Real Housewife of Beverly Hills.

Too bad, she wasn't shit but in-house pussy.

Although she was the father of my youngest son, I simply didn't have the same love or respect for her that I did for Khari. And while she was a down ass chick, and loyal to a fault, she couldn't hold a candle to my Khari.

"You back dumb early," I said, not looking up from the scale. That morning, I blessed her with a couple thousands to go shopping and get her hair done. I was forever spoiling her ass. I even bought her a new whip and a high-rise luxury apartment in the heart of Atlanta. As long as she stayed down, her loyalty would never go unrewarded. "Enjoyed yaself?"

"Absolutely. Thank you so much, baby. I really needed it," she said, patting her fresh weave.

"Mall must ain't have much new shit for you to buy. It don't even feel like you were gone that long."

Leah practically lived in that mothafucka. She spent so much money on clothes and shoes that we ran out of space in the walk-in closet, and that bitch was the size of a small studio apartment. She ended up having to use the spare bedroom as her second closet.

Growing up piss poor, I knew what it felt like to not have shit and I didn't want that for my family. I may've been a scumbag ass nigga, but I was a firm believer of taking care of my loved ones. Leah and Malik would never be without, and the same rang true for Khari and Ali.

"No. It wasn't that," Leah said. "Honestly, I rushed back home 'cuz I had started missing you."

"Oh yeah? And what'chu miss?"

Leah walked over and kissed me on the lips and grabbed my dick through my jeans. "You know I can't stay away from it for too long."

She ain't give a fuck about the guns and bricks that were laid out on the table waiting to be bust down. If it were Khari, she'd be losing her mothafucking mind. She ain't like our son being exposed to the street life. She wanted to protect him from it for as long as she could.

"Oh, you missed this dick, huh?" I slapped her big, juicy ass causing it to jiggle. Leah was chocolate, thick, and rocked a short haircut that suited the shape of her pretty ass face. She was bad than a mothafucka—but any bitch that I was affiliated with was. And best believe a nigga had high standards.

Leah smiled and licked her full lips. "I miss this dick all the time," she purred. "Even when it's in me..." She was beyond grateful that I was back in her life, and would do just about anything to make sure I didn't leave. She cooked, cleaned and sucked my dick like a porn star every morning faithfully.

Sometimes I asked myself why I never put a ring on her finger instead. Leah knew what came with this street shit and she respected it.

Pushing away the coke and scale, she

climbed on top of the table and lifted her dress, revealing the lace crotch-less panties underneath. My dick grew hard just looking at that pretty ass, peanut butter colored pussy. It was shaved completely bald, and the tiny piece of flesh between her lips, begging to be tasted.

"Damn, girl...Spread that pussy open," I whispered. "Lemme smell it."

Leah eagerly did as I asked, allowing me to take a generous whiff of her pink, slippery fortress. After probing it with my index, I sucked the juices off and lowered my head. *"Mmm...Lemme taste it."*

Leah's back arched as I closed my mouth over her sopping pussy and sucked on her bean like a piece of fruit. Spreading her thighs far apart, I ate her right there on the kitchen table like she was my last meal.

Thrusting her hips forward, she rode my tongue as if it were a tidal wave. "Oh my God!" she moaned, gripping the back of my head. "Aubrey, I fucking love you! I swear, I'll die for you."

I grabbed the 9 mm that was lying on the table, and started rubbing the cold steel against her clit. "You better mean that shit too, bitch. Don't play with me."

Leah yelped in pleasure after I slipped just the barrel of the gun inside. "Baby, I would never tell you anything I don't mean," she moaned. "I love you. I'll do anything for you, baby. I'm yours.

Use me how you want to."

Turned on by her submissiveness, I tongued her down aggressively. "Pull my dick out. I wanna use that asshole." Wrapping a hand around her throat, I started fucking her pussy with the gun faster and deeper while she fumbled with unbuttoning my jeans.

After freeing my anaconda, she gently stroked it in her small hand. I was about to bend her over the table when she dropped to her knees in front of me and stuffed my dick in her mouth.

If it was one thing this bitch knew, it was how to deep-throat a cock. Honestly, I think that's one of the main reasons I kept her around all these years. Leah sucked me like her life depended on it, like she didn't require oxygen. She sucked my dick so ferociously, you would've thought she was trying to suck the skin off that mothafucka. That's how hard she went.

Holding the back of her head, I watched as my dick disappeared and reappeared covered in thick saliva. Tears ran down her face and she had slobber all over her, but she didn't dare slow down. She knew how much I loved that wet ass, sloppy head. When she started licking my nuts, I almost lost it. I was so close to cumming that I could feel the pressure building up, so I snatched her to feet and bent her over the table. I wasn't 'bout to waste a nut on some head.

After spitting into the palm of my hand, I lathered my dick and jammed it deep into her tight asshole.

"*Unnhh!*" Leah shrieked in agony as I forced myself into her tiny hole. And though it was pure hell for her, it was heaven on Earth for me.

Khari never let me fuck her in the ass, but Leah was so desperate to keep me that she pretty much let me do anything to her body.

"*Unh!* Not...so hard, baby," Leah begged, pressing a hand against my leg. She barely had any time to brace herself before I put it in her body.

As fucked up as it was, I enjoyed seeing her in pain. The shit actually made my dick harder. It was the reason I enjoyed anal. "You my bitch," I said, pulling her hair. "Therefore you gon' take this dick how I give it."

I was just about to drill her shit when I heard the unmistakable sound of movement in the other room. Our son Malik was at his grandmother's, so I knew that it wasn't him roaming about. Therefore, it had to be an intruder.

"What's wrong...?" Leah asked, breathing hard. "Why'd you sto—"

"*Ssh!*" I quickly raised my hand to stop her from speaking. I wanted to be sure that I wasn't tripping. "I thought I heard someth—"

Suddenly, and out of nowhere, a group of masked men stormed the room and started spraying everything in sight.

TAT! TAT! TAT! TAT! TAT! TAT! TAT! TAT! TAT!

2

AUBREY

In horror, I watched as Leah took several shots to the chest that were without a doubt meant for me. Grabbing my pistol, I leapt behind the fridge for cover and let off several rounds of my own.

POP!

POP!

I managed to hit the nearest intruder right between the eyes, dropping his ass where he stood. I was hell-bent on killing every single last one of them cocksuckers. No way in hell them mothafuckas was leaving alive.

"You wan' fucking test me?! C'MON, PUSSY RAASCLAAT! I murder for fun!" I yelled in a thick Caribbean accent.

POP!

POP!

Gunfire lit up the room as we fired on each other.

POP!

POP!

"Nuh ramp wid mi! I MURDER FOR FUN, BLOODCLAAT!"

I didn't give a fuck about leaving one alive

to interrogate. I already knew the mothafucka that was behind this shit. And he and every last one of them was going down with him.

"*Cockroach nuh business inna fowl fite!*"

TAT! TAT! TAT! TAT! TAT! TAT! TAT! TAT! TAT!

The shooters lit up the walls, cabinets, and fridge in a desperate attempt to take me out. They were obviously out for blood, but ironically so was I. The war between Cue and I had just begun.

"*Emboscarle!*" one of the killers shouted in Spanish, instructing another to ambush me. Had it not been for the fact that my Bunkie was a Migo, I would've never understood them.

As soon as the nigga rounded the corner, I blew his eye out the back of his head. Two down, two to go.

"*PUSSY BUMBACLOT!*" I yelled arrogantly. "You come to my home! Kill my woman!" Tears filled my eyes as I looked at Leah's dead body stretched out on the floor, her body riddled with bullet holes that didn't even have her name on them. "Me no let'cha leave alive, batty bwoy! YA FUCKING HEAR ME!"

POP!

POP!

POP!

I continued to fire off shots until I suddenly

ran out of ammo.

"Shit!" I tossed the meaningless weapon to the floor in anger.

With limited options at my disposal, I ran full speed towards the floor to ceiling windows and launched my body through it, shattering the glass on impact. The seven story plunge ended with me landing on top of a closed dumpster lid. I hit the surface hard before uncontrollably falling to the ground. I felt like I had dislocated my fucking back but at least it broke my fall.

Limping to my feet, I took off running away from the building. My car was across the street in the parking garage, so I figured the sooner I got to it the safer I'd be. I needed medical attention and time to regroup.

Sadly, I was so focused on getting away that I didn't even notice the car coming straight at me.

3

KHARI

The moment I spotted Aubrey's trifling ass, I mashed my foot down onto the accelerator, increasing my speed. To be honest, it was my first reaction. When I looked at him, all I saw was a nigga that had gotten my son shot and imprisoned the love of my life.

Aubrey's actions had left me infuriated— to the point where I couldn't even think straight. So when I saw him, I did what any woman that was fed up and in my predicament would do. I ran his ass over with my fucking car.

WHOOMP!

Krrrrrr!

Aubrey's body hit the hood of the car, shattering the windshield upon impact. I'd hit him so hard that he went flying into a parked minivan.

Regret set in as soon as I realized what I'd done.

Oh my God.

Why did I just do that stupid shit?

What the fuck was I thinking?

I began to panic as thoughts of me in a prison cell crept into my mind. The last thing I wanted was to lose custody of my child, all because I couldn't control my rage. Aubrey had just made me so fucking angry. I'd had enough of his bullshit, and when I caught him in the middle of the street, I just saw red. In that split moment, I forgot about everything—including consequences.

After looking in my rearview and noticing that he wasn't moving, I began to panic even more. *What the hell am I gonna do if he's dead? I don't want a fucking murder charge.* Apart of me felt like peeling out, but I knew the Christian thing to do was to check on him.

Swallowing my fear, I put my car in park and climbed out. A few nearby pedestrians were already making their way over as well.

"Oh my God!" I gasped and covered my mouth once I saw the bone sticking out of his right leg. He was in bad shape, and from where I stood, it didn't look like he was breathing either. "Somebody call for help!" I cried. "Oh my God, Aubrey, I'm so sorry! I'm so sorry!" I graciously apologized for my reckless actions. "What the fuck is wrong with me?!"

Two of the bystanders quickly pulled their phones out to call 911—but out nowhere, Aubrey rose from the dead.

I barely had a chance to celebrate before bullets suddenly started whizzing past my head.

TAT! TAT! TAT! TAT! TAT! TAT! TAT! TAT! TAT!

Before I could realize what was happening,

Aubrey grabbed me and pulled me behind the van in just the nick of time. Had I been standing a second longer, I would've been shot in the head.

TAT! TAT! TAT! TAT! TAT! TAT! TAT! TAT! TAT!

Cars and innocent bystanders were struck by the rapid gunfire of machine guns. I was only there to confront Aubrey, but apparently I'd stepped into an all-out war zone.

Oh my God. I don't wanna die.

"I ain't finna let shit happen to you!" Aubrey yelled over the gunshots.

I didn't even realize that I'd said it aloud. That's just how terrified I was. All I could think about Ali and the fact that I didn't even tell him I loved him before storming out to look for Aubrey.

"Keep your head down," he instructed. "We gon' make a run for the car—"

"No!" I bellowed. "I can't do it! I—I can't!"

"Khari,   look   at   me!"
"I can't breathe!" I said, hyperventilating. I'd never been in a more frightening and stressful situation. Once again, I had allowed myself to be caught up in Aubrey's bullshit ass antics.

"Look at me, Khari!" he repeated.

This time I did as he asked.

"Keep your head down and stay behind me, okay!"

"Alright."

Holding onto the back of his shirt, I followed him as he limped towards my car. Luckily, it was only a few feet away.

Once we reached it, we jumped in and skirted off. The back window was shot out as I hastily rounded the corner and I ducked out of fear.

"Go, Khari! This bitch can't go any faster!" Aubrey yelled.

"I'm flooring it! What the fuck do you expect? It's a Ford! Not a fucking Ferrari!"

"What happened to ya other whip?"

"Your bitch sabotaged my brake lines and nearly killed my mama, remember?"

Aubrey immediately fell silent.

There was a long, deep gash along his cheek from where a bullet had grazed him.

I decided to change the topic to a more important one. "Are they still behind us?"

Aubrey craned his neck to check. "Nah. Them niggas was on foot so we got a bit of a head start."

"Who the fuck were they?" I asked him. "And why were they shooting at you?"

"That's a question for ya boy," he sneered.

Now it was my turn to fall silent. I would've

never guessed that Cue was somehow involved.

"Damn...my fucking leg is killing me," he groaned.

"I'll take you the hospital—"

"No!" Aubrey quickly said. "That'll only lead to more problems for me. I don't need the fucking police involved."

"Well, where do you want me to take you?"

"I gotta boy out in Marietta that'll patch me up. For now, just head in that direction."

I did as I was told, only out of the gratitude in my heart for him saving my life.

"You still keep that burner in the stash?" Aubrey asked, opening the glove compartment.

He'd taught me a while back to never migrate without protection. "Of course."

After retrieving my loaded pistol, he checked to see how many rounds there were and switched the safety off.

All of a sudden, and without warning, he put the gun to my temple.

4

KHARI

Aubrey cocked the hammer. "Bitch, I could blow yo' mothafucking head off."

The pressure of having a gun to my skull caused me to swerve a little. "And I should've killed your stupid ass when I hit you, but I didn't. So if you ain't gon' use that thing, I suggest you get it out my fucking face!"

He kept the gun aimed at me for several seconds before finally lowering it. That's when I hauled off and punched him in his leg, causing him to wince in pain.

"HAVE YOU LOST YO' MOTHAFUCKING MIND?! Don't you ever put a gun in my face again! For God's sake, Aubrey, I'm the mother of your child!" I rolled my eyes. "Not that that's ever kept you from disrespecting me—"

"Bitch, I'm two seconds away from putting a bullet in yo' head. Now shut the fuck up and drive. Please," he added.

The remainder of the ride was silent and tension-filled. There was so much shit I wanted to say to Aubrey, but for some reason I couldn't figure out how to word it. And with the way he was waving that pistol around, I was unsure if I even wanted to.

Besides, every time I fixed my mouth up to

speak, I found myself on the verge of cursing his ass out—and I knew that would only lead to more outrage. Honestly, I didn't think he'd shoot me but I wasn't about to risk testing him either.

Twenty minutes later, we finally arrived at the private medical center located just outside the city. "Pull around to the back," Aubrey instructed.

I carefully did as he asked before switching the gears to park.

When he struggled to climb out the car, I didn't even bother to offer my help. In my opinion, he didn't get shit he didn't already have coming. Aubrey had done so much foul shit, that I wasn't even surprised his past was coming back to haunt him. Evidently, someone out there wanted him dead just as bad as I did. And for once, I couldn't quite say that I felt any sympathy for him.

Karma had finally caught up to him.

After watching him successfully climb out, I prepared to take off but Aubrey quickly stopped me. "Where the fuck you think you going?" he asked.

"I took you where you needed to go. There's no reason for me to stick around, so I'm leaving—"

"Bitch, you leave when I say you can fucking leave. Now get'cho ass out the fucking car 'fore I drag you up out that mufucka."

It took for him to point his gun again to

make me finally move. Sucking my teeth, I opened the door and climbed out the car. Without asking, Aubrey used my shoulder as a crutch as we headed into the building.

As soon as walked in, medical personnel rushed over to get Aubrey onto a gurney. I followed them at a distance as they led him to an operating room. Inside, was a doctor already prepped and awaiting our arrival. Because he was wearing a surgical mask, the only thing I could identify was that he was a white male.

"Shit," he murmured, staring at the protruding bone. "I'm not gonna bullshit with you. This will hurt like hell."

Aubrey frowned. "Damn, Doc. You could've lied a little."

Taking in a deep breath, he braced himself for the pain sure to come.

The moment he snapped his bone back in place, Aubrey screamed and I keeled over and threw up.

"Damn, Doc. That was much worse than I thought it'd be."

As I wiped my lips, I noticed that Aubrey was looking at me suspiciously. "What the fuck was that?"

"The blood and everything—it just made me nauseous."

Aubrey gave me a doubtful stare. "You *sure*

that's the only reason you nauseous?"

I picked up on his tone immediately and became offended. "What are you getting at?"

"You tell me. Matter fact. Let's put the speculation to rest and do a test while we're here."

"But, Aubrey, your leg. You can't be serious."

"I'm dead ass. And this shit ain't up for debate. I need to know right now if you carrying that nigga's seed."

After being stitched and bandaged, Aubrey forced me to pee in a cup so that it could be tested. The half-hour wait for the results felt like an eternity, especially since Aubrey was hovering over me the entire time like a dark cloud.

I said a silent prayer to myself that I wasn't. With all the crazy shit happening lately, having another baby was the last thing I needed on my plate. One was enough. When the doctor finally handed Aubrey the results, I held my breath and hoped for a favorable outcome.

Aubrey took one look at the paper and went berserk.

WHAP!

He slapped me upside the head with his gun so hard that it caused my head to snap violently to the right. I'd never been hit so hard in my life. "YOU FUCKING BITCH! How could you do this shit to me?!" he screamed, throwing the piece of paper at me.

I started crying hysterically as blood trickled down my face. I was so afraid that I couldn't even speak. I was used to Aubrey's blustery explosions of rage, but this was a whole new level of anger. I'd never seen him this upset in all our eight years of being together.

"You were supposed to wait for me! Not get knocked up by some nigga while I'm behind bars, hustling for you and our family!" He slapped me again. "What the fuck is in your head, bitch? Huh? Answer me!"

"Stop hitting me!"

WHAP!

Suddenly, Aubrey slapped me to the floor. "You dirty, backstabbing cunt! You better get rid of that mothafucka before I do it for you! I'll be damned if you give that nigga a baby! YOU GOT ME FUCKED UP!" he yelled. "All the shit I do—All the shit I sacrificed, and this is how you repay me?! By letting some fuck nigga stick his raw dick in you!" Spit flew out his mouth as he hollered and ranted. "Bitch, I could beat the baby out'cho mothafucking ass!"

It felt like déjà vu all over again as I cowered in the corner, shielding my face from any incoming attacks. Aubrey was a loose cannon.

How the hell did I get into this chaotic heap of relationship drama, I asked myself?

"Man... Get the fuck out of here, Khari," he said. "I can't even stand to look at you right now. It makes me fucking sick. If I stare at you a second longer, I'm liable to choke the life out'cho stupid ass. Man, just go. Get the fuck out. Now."

I quickly scurried to my feet and ran towards the door before changed his mind and started beating on me again.

"Oh, and Khari?" Aubrey stopped me just before I walked out. "That mothafucka won't see the light of day. I can promise you that. Them bars won't protect him from what the fuck I got planned. You can believe that shit."

His chilling threat left me shook and wondering just how far he'd go to prove a point.

5

KYLIE

"All rise."

Wiping my sweaty palms on the fabric of my dress pants, I stood to my feet and faced the judge presiding over my case. Among the attendees were Mama and her boyfriend Larry. I expected Khari to be there as well, but I didn't see her face in the crowd of people. I figured something important must've came up, otherwise she would've made it. It wasn't like my sister to not be there for me when I needed her.

I hope everything's okay.

Word had quickly spread that Aubrey was released, and I could only imagine the type of drama that would cause.

"Where the hell is Tino?" I mumbled in frustration. He also said that he would be here, but like my sister, he was missing in action.

"Department One of the Superior Court is now in session. Honorable Lee M. Dupree presiding. Please be seated."

Everyone in the courtroom sat back down as the judge took his seat behind the raised desk. "Good morning, ladies and gentlemen. Calling the case of the People of the State of Georgia versus Kylie. Are both sides ready?"

I quickly turned to face my lawyer. He looked more nervous than I did, but prepared nonetheless. Pushing his glasses up on the bridge of his nose, he nodded his head and grabbed his files. "Yes, your honor."

The prosecutor shot me a nasty look before answering. "Yes, your honor." They were determined to see me tossed in a cell for at least two decades of my life. A punishment that was certainly not worth the risk of spending counterfeit cash.

If I had never involved myself with Jamaal and his schemes, I wouldn't even be here, facing this dilemma. *That bitch should be right here where I'm standing. Not me.* It was his fucking fault that I got caught up in the first place. Now I was facing up to 20 years for intentional fraud.

Scanning the crowd of attendees, I noticed that he wasn't among them. Honestly, I didn't know whether to be happy or pissed about it. *That nigga faker than the cash he had me spending*, I told myself. It seemed like the moment I got arrested, he turned his back on me. And then to add insult to injury, he fucked my best friend.

If they convict me, I swear I'm putting a bullet in that nigga's head. He damn sure deserved it.

My homicidal thoughts were interrupted by the judge. "Will the clerk please swear in the jury?"

The entire jury stood and raised their hand, swearing to give a truthful verdict according to the evidence. Once they were seated, court was underway.

"Your Honor—and ladies and gentlemen of the jury, the defendant has been charged with intentional fraud and use of counterfeit money." The prosecutor then brandished a folder containing copies of all my receipts. "The evidence will show that the defendant has purchased more than $350,000 worth of merchandise," he said, causing everyone in the courtroom to gasp at the staggering amount. "The evidence I present will prove to you that the defendant is guilty as charged."

My lawyer quickly came to my defense. "Your Honor and ladies and gentlemen of the jury under the law, my client is presumed innocent until *proven* guilty. During this trial, you will hear no real evidence against my client. You will come to know the truth. That Kylie was unintentionally using counterfeit money—"

"Which is still very much illegal!" the prosecutor butted in.

"Yes, but a court will only charge someone with fraud if it is proven that the individual consciously tried to pass fake money off as real currency—and I can assure that my client did that unknowingly. Therefore, my client is innocent."

"For now," the prosecutor shot back.

"The prosecution may call its first witness," the judge said.

Rolling my eyes in disgust, I watched as the clerk from the casino approached the stand. She was a short, pudgy black woman who wore her hair in long crochet braids. She was there the day that I was arrested and I knew nothing she had to say would be in my favor.

"Please stand and raise your right hand," the clerk instructed. "Do you promise that the testimony you shall give in the case before this court shall be the truth, the whole truth, and nothing but the truth, so help you God?"

"I do," she stated.

"Please state your first and last name."

"Marissa Campbell."

"Marissa, where do you work?"

"At the MGM Hotel and Casino in Vegas."

For five minutes, Marissa ranted about the reckless way I spent money and how she knew for a fact that it was counterfeit. Apparently, she was the one who'd alerted the authorities. She painted me out to be a villain and was among those who wanted to see me behind bars.

When she finally climbed down from the stand, I was grateful that her turn had ended. "Damn. I thought us sistas was supposed to stick together," I said as she walked past me.

"Don't try that sista bullshit with me. I stand by fairness. Not by fraud."

"You need to stand on a treadmill, you fat snitch ass bitch!"

The judge immediately started banging his gavel. "Order in the courtroom!" he yelled. "Outbursts like that will not be tolerated!"

After everyone finally settled down, we continued with the trial. It lasted for over three hours, and the jury still wasn't able to come to a verdict—which meant we would have to reschedule. Luckily, that granted me just a bit more time with my family and loved ones. With the way things were looking now, I wasn't sure how much longer I'd have my freedom.

On my way out the courtroom, I noticed a familiar face in the hallway. *Unbe-fucking-lievable*.

"You gotta lot nerve coming here," I told Jamaal.

"How did it go?" he asked.

"Nigga, how you think it went? The prosecutor ran wild on my ass. If I'm convicted, I could be looking at twenty years."

"You ain't gon' get convicted," he said.

"You don't know that," I said, brushing past him.

Jamaal quickly grabbed my elbow from behind to stop me. "C'mon, Kylie. We can't keep doing this shit. At some point, we need to talk."

"I don't need to do shit—but stay away from fuck niggas like you! You've done nothing but cause me trouble!"

"Bitch, you act like I put a fucking gun to yo' head! Ain't nobody force you to spend that cash—"

"Oh, don't give me that bullshit, Jamaal. You knew how bad I needed that money and you took advantage of me. Plain and simple," I told him. "I didn't ask for all this shit! How would *you* feel if you were the one being accused of something you knew you didn't do?"

Jamaal shrugged casually. "Shit, I'm accused every day I walk out the door as a black man—"

"Oh, cut the act, Jamaal. That victim bullshit ain't gon' work on me."

He pulled me close. "Well, what *will* work on you?"

I quickly pushed him off. "You dropping dead. Or leaving me the fuck alone for the rest of my life. Either or will do just fine."

Before he could respond, my phone started ringing. The number that was calling me was from an unrecognizable number. I thought about ignoring it, but decided to answer instead. With Khari still MIA, I figured it was probably important.

"Hello?"

"Kylie...it's me, Touché." His deep voice filled the receiver. "Look, I hate to call you so abruptly like this...but I got some bad news, baby girl. Is there any way we can speak in person?"

My heart immediately dropped into the pit of my stomach. I just knew that something had happened to Tino.

6

TOUCHÉ

I made sure to put on my game face as I headed to Kylie's place to give her the news. I'd just got back from DC this morning after paying a visit to Tino's baby mama—who didn't take the news well at all.

Now that their daughter was without a father, she was worried about how that would affect their future and finances. I was able to put her mind at ease a little when I offered to step up to the plate in his place. I mean shit, he *was* my boy. The least I could do was take care of the funeral and his family. If the shoe were on the other foot, I knew he'd do the same for me.

Tino was my nigga; hell, we'd practically grown up together. But the day that he chose to affiliate himself with the enemy, he pretty much sealed his fate. It wasn't easy to pull the trigger on a longtime friend, but I felt betrayed by the fact that he'd allied himself with the enemy. And what was even worse was that he'd left me in the dark about the shit.

Back at the club, before the shooting, he looked me dead in the eyes and said he'd handle Cue. But instead, he partnered up with the mothafucka, turning his back on the niggas who'd been in his corner since day 1. Tino's greed and lack of loyalty had ultimately killed him.

As I pulled up to Kylie's house, an unsettling feeling took over me. It was the same feeling I had when I went to see Tino's baby mama. After turning off the engine, I climbed out my copper tone McLaren and approached her house.

On the way to the door, I lit a blunt in order to calm my nerves. To be real, I was a bit on edge. It wasn't easy for me to look her in the face and lie—mainly because I'd been secretly feeling her for some time now.

Whenever she was around me, I got anxious. She'd always had that effect on me, and she didn't even know it. Had it not been for the fact that she was Tino's girl, I would've been made a move long ago.

As soon as I reached her door, I ashed the blunt and banged her line. Kylie answered on the second ring in a somewhat shaky tone. "Hey, Touché." I could tell her nerves were just as bad as mine.

"Aye, I'm outside," I told her.

"Okay. Here I come." Kylie hung up the phone and a few seconds later, the front door slowly opened.

As soon as I saw her, I noticed how different she looked. In addition to the weight lost, she had faint bags under her eyes that indicated a lack of sleep. Kylie wasn't her normal, vibrant self, and it didn't take a genius to see that she was stressed.

Suddenly, I felt bad for being the one to have to add more to her plate. "Kylie...I...Uh...is it okay if I come in?"

Kylie stepped to the side to allow me entrance. I couldn't even look her in the eyes as I prepared to feed her some bullshit excuse about Tino's death. "Kylie...I don't know how to say this—"

"Just say it. It's about Tino, right?" Her voice cracked with emotion as she spoke. "He's dead, isn't he?"

The long pause that followed her question told her everything she needed to know. Clamping a hand over her mouth, she gasped in sorrow. Tears quickly filled her eyes and I didn't know whether to console her or give her space.

"How?" she asked.

Scratching the back of my ear out of habit, I prepared to tell her the same story I'd told his baby mama. "Some niggas we were beefin' with shot him in the hospital. I gotta feelin' it was the same mothafuckas who ran up in the club."

Upon hearing the tragic news, Kylie collapsed into my arms and started crying hysterically. Holding her close, I tried my best to console her while ignoring the fact that she felt so good in my arms.

"I can't even hear this shit right now. I just

don't believe that! We were just together that night! I was just with him!" she sobbed. "I don't even think I got to tell him I love him the last time I saw him!"

I rubbed her back in a soothing manner. "I'm sure he knew, K."

Burying her face in my chest, she cried even harder. Kylie didn't know it, but she was crying for the both of us. Not only did I lose my best friend. I lost a brother.

7

KHARI

After the crazy ass encounter with my ex-fiancé, I decided to stop by Mama's to check on Kylie and see how the trial went. I was supposed to be there, but with everything that'd happened with Cue and Aubrey, I had gotten sidetracked.

"Kylie's probably pissed at me," I said, pulling into her driveway.

Ali perked up in the backseat when he realized we were at his grandma's. She spoiled him senselessly, so he got excited every time we came to visit. I had just picked him up from school, and I was grateful that he didn't question me about the broken window or the dent on the hood of the car. I still had a hard time believing just that afternoon I was being shot at.

After pulling into Mama's driveway, I turned the car off and hopped out with my son. He was growing so fast in such a short amount of time. At eight years old, he damn near came to my chest.

All of a sudden, I missed him being a baby. A small smile formed on my lips as I recalled the life growing inside of me. Although I had mixed feelings about the pregnancy, I couldn't deny that it was nice to have a second chance at motherhood.

As soon as I reached the door, it swung open and Touché swaggered out like he paid the bills there. Naturally, I immediately found myself on the defensive. Grabbing my son, I pulled him close, shielding him from the bastard that I just knew was affiliated with Aubrey someway somehow. Call it a mother's tuition...but I just didn't trust Touché—and I couldn't wait to get in my sister's ass about having him over.

Touché gave us a sympathetic look, opened his mouth to speak, and then quickly closed it. I figured he didn't have a damn thing to say because he walked off, climbed in his car, and pulled off.

Barging inside the house, I immediately went to Kylie's room, where I found her curled up on the bed with her knees drawn to her chest. Tears were running down her face as she lay in a fetal position.

"Tino was killed," she cried.

"Kylie! Oh my God!" I covered my mouth in shock, floored by the news. I knew that Tino was involved in some heavy shit, but I didn't know to what extent. Apparently, he was in too deep. "I'm sorry. I'm so sorry," I said, rushing to her side. "I know how much he meant to you."

Kylie sniffled and looked at me with teary eyes. I had never seen my sister so distraught. "You know what? Sometimes I don't think *he* ever knew just *how* much."

"Trust me. I'm sure he did."

More tears escaped from Kylie's puffy, red eyes. "First the shit with Jamaal and now this." She shook her head. "It feels like my love life's cursed."

I rubbed her back as she vented. "Now you know that's not true. Tino was involved in the street life. And with the street life, death is just inevitable."

"How did you and Aubrey last so long with you knowing that?"

I snorted. "I wouldn't quite say we lasted."

Kylie shook her head. "You know what I mean."

"Yeah...I know what you mean."

Kylie continued to stare off into space as I rubbed her back. "I just don't understand, sis. I mean, I know that he's gone but...I'm just so fucking confused. I don't even know how to feel. I'm mostly angry at myself for even getting caught up. If I had never involved myself with a nigga like him, it wouldn't hurt this bad."

"Sis, it's gonna hurt," I said truthfully. "But you can't regret the time you two spent together. You were happy with him and I know you were. So don't go beating yourself up. You can't change what's happened. But you can be grateful that you got to know a guy like him."

Kylie started crying harder. "He was a great guy too, Khari. He really was. Underneath that hard ass façade he put on, he was a real sweetheart."

"I know he was." There was a brief pause on my end. "Look, sis, I gotta tell you something. I don't know how well you know that nigga that just left the house or what type of connection ya'll got, but I think it's best if you stay away from him. I don't have a good feeling about that dude at all."

Kylie quickly put some distance between us. Apparently, she didn't appreciate me speaking my mind at a time like this. "I think I just wanna be alone for now, Khari." It was clear she didn't want to hear anything else I had to say because she was pushing me away. That seemed to be my sister's favorite thing to do.

"Okay...I'll give you your space. But just please...*please*, heed my warning," I begged. "It's for your own safety. Stay away from that dude. He's bad news."

8

KYLIE

ONE WEEK LATER

Tino's funeral was held at *Ebenezer Baptist Church* on Auburn Avenue, just a few blocks from the great Martin Luther King Jr.'s childhood home. The service was so packed that they had to put chairs out on the front lawn just to accommodate the many guests.

Tino knew a lot of people, and most of them were sad to see him go—especially me. Dressed in all black, I showed up alone to pay my respects. Thankfully, Touché was able to get me a seat in the front pew with his closest friends and family members, so that I wouldn't have to sit outside.

Tino's mother and baby mama shot me several nasty looks, as if my mere presence was offensive to them. *Why the fuck these bitches keep staring at me*, I asked myself? You'd think I was the one who murdered him.

The only reason I knew who they were was because I'd stumbled across a photo album in Tino's home. He looked just like his mother, except she had a darker complexion and was heavy set. His baby mama was gorgeous enough to make me question why he left her in the first place. She was caramel-colored with hazel eyes and naturally beautiful features. She reminded me of a younger Tyra Banks.

I wonder how they know who I am. I figured that Touché must've told them.

Disregarding the hateful looks they tossed my way, I made my way to Tino's casket to say my final goodbye. It wasn't until I saw him lying in the plush bedding of the casket that I realized he was actually gone—forever.

This shit is not happening?

This was not how things was supposed to end.

Hovering over his casket, I stared at the stiff, suited, hollow shell of the man I once loved. "Why, Tino?" I asked in a quiet tone. "Why did you leave me? I needed you." Tears snaked down my cheeks as I reached out and touched his cold, lifeless hand. "I needed you, Tino...more than the streets needed you...more than you knew. How could you leave me like this? This was not how our story was supposed to end, baby." Leaning down, I pressed a delicate kiss on his forehead. "Until we meet again. I love you, Terentino."

***

After Tino's funeral, I attended the repass that was held at the house he used to live in. There were so many people there that it looked like we were having a block party. People were cooking, laughing, talking, and reminiscing about the good times they shared with Tino. Instead of mourning his absence, we were celebrating his life.

I was staring at the children playing in the front lawn, when his baby mama came out of nowhere and interrupted my daydreaming. "Kylie, right?"

Removing my dark shades, I looked up at her in surprise that she was actually speaking to me. During the entire funeral, she'd been casting awkward glances so I didn't know what to expect. I damn sure didn't think she'd fix her mouth up to talk to me.

"Yeah."

"Can I sit next to you?" she asked.

"Go right ahead." I scooted over on the front steps of the home so that she could take a seat. "I never got your name, by the way."

"Ashley. And that's Taylor," she said, pointing to her three-year old daughter. She was horse-playing with the other children on the front lawn. She was spitting image of her father. And while it was nice to see the little having fun, I knew that it was because she was too young to understand what was going on.

"I can't believe he's really gone," she said.

"I can't believe it either," I said. "It's funny. We take shit for granted until it's gone. Life can change so quick in just the blink of an eye." I shook my head. "I never saw this coming."

"I wish I could say you and me both. But I knew it'd only be a matter of time. When you lived the type of life Tino did, you're bound to end up in the ground sooner or later. Unfortunately for him, it was sooner than any of us anticipated." There was another awkward silence before she spoke again. "You know, I'm not gonna lie. When I first saw you at the wake, I was pretty pissed about you being there."

I quickly cut my eyes at her after hearing that shit. I was just about to tell her about herself, but she quickly explained what she meant by her statement. "But then I had to put my jealousy aside and remind myself that you loved him— probably just as much as I did." She paused. "I say all this to say, if you ever need to talk to someone, feel free to reach out to me anytime."

Her offer took me by surprise. I was expecting her to say something ignorant, not to extend her friendship. "Okay, um, thanks. The same goes for you."

Ashley surprised me again by reaching out and hugging me. "Don't worry. We'll get through this." It sounded like she was trying to convince herself more than she was me. I didn't know about her, but it would take me an eternity before I got over Tino's death. Now that he was gone, nothing would ever be the same.

"Aye, Kylie? Can I holla at'chu for a second?" Touché asked.

"Yeah...sure." Standing to my feet, I followed him inside the house. The place was packed with people wall-to-wall, who were competing to get a plate. *Black folk don't know how to act when it comes to soul food*, I thought.

Walking past the horde of people, Touché led me to the empty den, before closing the doors behind us. It was the only place we could talk in private since the house was filled to capacity. "How you holding up?" he asked.

I sighed deeply. "Well...I'm holding...the best I can."

Touché closed the space between us a little. "I just wanna tell you, like I told T's baby mama, if it's anything you need—anything at all—I got'chu. Tino ain't have no will or no shit like that, but I know he'd want me to look out. And it's the least I could do—"

"Touché, thanks. I appreciate it. I really do...but I don't wanna impose—"

"You ain't imposing." He took my hands in his. "Trust me. I wanna take care of you."

There was something about the way he was looking into my eyes while caressing my hand that made me feel uneasy. Like he was coming onto me, and considering the circumstances, I didn't find it appropriate.

Snatching my hand away, I cleared my throat nervously. "Um...Thank you," I said, not bothering to make eye contact. Instead, I looked at the floor as if it would speak back to me. "Is that all you wanted to tell me?"

Touché gently tilted my chin up so that he could look into my eyes. "There's more I wanna say...but I'm afraid now ain't the best time to."

I could smell the Henny seeping from his pores as he spoke. He was drunk and probably high too. He lost his best friend so I expected that much. What I didn't expect was him blatantly coming onto me. "Well, that's probably for the best..."

Touché chuckled and let his hand drop. "My bad. I—uh...I can only imagine how I'm coming off to you right now." He ran a palm over his fresh cut. "Don't hold it against me though. I gotta couple drinks in my system. Sometimes it makes me have a loose tongue."

"Well, you know what they say," I told him. "A drunk man's talk is a sober man's thoughts."

Touché was quiet after I put him on blast.

"Look...I get it...we're both in a vulnerable place right now. I lost my boyfriend. You lost your best friend. But let's not do anything rash—"

All of a sudden, and without warning, Touché leaned in and kissed me.

9

KHARI

It was a quarter after five when I walked in my house with several grocery bags from Kroger. I'd promised Ali that I would make him tacos, so I had to go and grab all of the essentials.

As soon as I entered my home, I noticed that candles were lit and soft R&B music was playing. Faith Evans "*I Love You*" poured through the entertainment system in the living room.

My heart belongs to you...

So what could I do...

To make you feel I'm down with...

You see me hangin around...

But you don't know how you make me feel for you...

And each and every day, I try to make some sense of this...

What you mean to me, I know it could be serious...

Each and every night, I dream about just holding you...

Loving you like this, what is a girl supposed to do...

I love you...

I want you...

You're the one that I live for...

And I can't take it any more...

Placing the bags down, I headed towards the living room, expecting to find my son and babysitter. What I found instead was the last person I expected to see. "Cue...?" His name left my lips in a breathless whisper. He turned around after hearing me walk in and smiled at me.

It felt like I was staring at a ghost. I couldn't believe that he was standing there in the flesh. "Am I dreaming?" I felt foolish asking but it seemed too good to be true.

"Come kiss me and find out..."

He didn't have to ask twice as I rushed towards him and flung my arms around his neck. The kiss he gave me was both passionate and aggressive, and I could tell he missed me just as much as I missed him. A few days apart felt like a few lifetimes.

"Oh my God! I can't believe you're really here! I thought I'd lost you!"

"You never gon' lose me, baby."

First time I saw your face...

My heart just erased...

All the guys I knew before...you walked into my life...

I touched and caressed his face as if I still

doubted he was real. "What—when—How'd you get out?"

Cue gave a dimpled grin. "C'mon now. You know you can't keep a good man down." Knowing him, he wouldn't give up the details so easily so I decided to drop the subject for now.

"Where's Ali and the babysitter?"

"Don't worry. I took care of it. Just for today, I want you all to myself." He pulled me close and kissed me again. "What happened to your face?" he asked, noticing the faint bruise on my cheek. He lightly ran the tips of his fingers across the tender spot.

"I—it's nothing. I bumped my head reaching for something under the sink."

Cue kissed my bruise, then the tip of my nose, then my lips. I moaned a little when his tongue snaked inside my mouth. He tasted like peppermint and smelled of Tom Ford French Vanille.

"I've missed you like crazy, baby," I whispered.

"And I missed the fuck out of you." Cue hoisted me up and I wrapped my legs around his waist. "Now lemme show you." He carried me to the bedroom as Faith continued to serenade us.

When we reached our room, he gently placed me down onto the cushy mattress. Admiring his toned physique, I watched as he slowly undressed first. With his bulging muscles and abs, he looked every bit like a Greek God.

Damn, I can't believe this is mine. I'd spent the better part of my life dreaming about this moment.

Looking up into his eyes, I ran my hand along his chest before allowing my tongue to follow. If I had my way, I'd lick every inch of his body. After I unzipped his pants, I pulled out 10 inches of rock hard steel. Just the sight of his big dick made my mouth water.

Cue released a deep groan as I struggled to fit every single last inch inside. For some reason, I was feeling friskier than normal. Perhaps, because it was because I thought I'd never see him again. Now that he was here, I just wanted to make him feel good. Unlike any woman ever had and ever would.

"Damn, K."

I could tell he wasn't used to me putting this much effort into pleasing him. I was sucking his dick so vigorously, that I gagged several times. The tip touched my tonsils; I was determined to swallow him whole.

"Shit, Khari. You gon' make me cum."

Not wanting him to bust so soon, I decided to move to his nuts. Cue practically lost his composure.

"Enough of this. I need to be inside you," he

said, pushing me back on the bed. "Wait, you—
Unhhhhh!" My sentence was cut off after he plunged deep inside of me. "Cue! *God!*" I moaned.

He had me breathing hard and struggling to keep up with the powerful strokes he delivered. One leg was hoisted over his shoulder while he fucked me in an upright position. The angle he was hitting it at allowed him to go deeper than normal. So deep that he was touching the depths of my stomach.

"Oh my goodness, baby! Damn!" I cried out. "Get that shit, baby! Get that shit! Fuck me like you missed me."

Hearing me say that made him start tapping my spot. "You like that?"

"Baby, I love it. Don't stop."

Cue started sucking on my toes. "I ain't gon' stop 'til you tell me to."

After wetting his finger, he began to play with my clit, bringing me closer and closer to my climax.

"Cue...I don't ever want you to leave me," I moaned.

Resting between my legs in a missionary position, he kissed me with an intense desire. "I never will, baby." He kissed my collarbone. "I'mma marry the shit outta you. That's what I'mma do." He kissed and licked on my neck, causing my leg to shiver and toes to curl. Just the sound of his voice made me wetter.

He had me strung out over his dick game. I was junkie for Cue's love. "Oh my God, baby! I'm 'bout to cum!" I bellowed. My cheeks flushed as a wave of ecstasy took over me.

"That's it." He kissed and nibbled on my chin. "Cum on yo' dick."

Shortly after, I felt him release his load deep inside me. For several seconds, he stayed planted right there while kissing me ever so passionately.

"I love you, Khari."

"I love you too, Cue. But we need to talk—primarily about your little *career*."

He hung his head in shame, knowing this moment would come sooner or later. "You're right," he agreed. "We do need to talk."

"And I want you to be one hundred percent honest with me—about everything," I added.

"I don't know how to be any other way," he said. "So where do I start?"

"How 'bout at the very beginning. And don't leave out *any* details."

10

TOUCHÉ

I was at the bar, tossing back shots when my line suddenly rang. It was a little after 2 a.m., so my first thought was that it was business-related. No one banged my line this late except Nicole, and that was only when she wanted some side nigga dick.

I'd dropped that crazy bitch months ago, so if it was her she could talk to the mothafucking voicemail. I ain't have shit to say to that ho. All she ever wanted to do was argue and fight anyway, like she ain't already have a mothafucking husband at home for that.

I ain't need that headache right now.

Much to my surprise, it wasn't Nicole hitting me up. It was Kylie.

Needless to say, I didn't expect to hear from her so soon—or ever, for that matter. After kissing her at Tino's repass, she fled the place like it was engulfed in flames. Drunk and high off meds, I did some stupid ass, impulsive shit without thinking. Although I was attracted to her, I wasn't in my right state of mind at the time. It wasn't my intentions to run her off. Honestly, I'd only wanted to console her. I never meant for shit to escalate so quickly and unexpectedly.

I wonder what made her reach out to me,

and so late at that...

Gathering my composure, I cleared my throat and answered. "Wassup, K...everything good?" There was a hint of concern in my voice. I didn't know what to expect.

"Yes and no...I can't sleep. Truthfully, I haven't been able to since I got the news," she said. "I was wondering if I could talk to you?"

"Shit, no doubt. You want me to come to you or—"

"No. I can come to you," she quickly said.

I had a feeling her people must've said something about me, which was why she didn't want me to come through. Why else would she turn me away so fast?

"Aight. I'mma shoot you a text. Meet me there in thirty."

"Alright."

After hanging up, I downed my shot off the Henny, and tipped the sexy ass bartender that I'd promised to wait for until her shift ended. She had a pouty look on her face since I was leaving sooner. But if I had to choose between her and Kylie, I'd choose Kylie every time.

She was my boy's girl, and it was dead ass wrong to be lusting after her the way that I was, but I couldn't help. Kylie was the forbidden fruit and I desperately wanted a taste of her. Hell, even a sample.

11

KYLIE

I couldn't believe that at 3 a.m. I was high on Percocets and on my way to see Touché. After Tino's death, I had started popping pills again and stealing. They were the only things that could help me cope through such difficult times.

I'd told Touché that I wanted to talk, but the truth was, he reminded me of Tino. Maybe because they were best friends. Every time that I looked at him, I saw Tino. Hell, even when he talked, I heard him. Touché reminded me so much of Tino that I found myself drawn to him.

I know it was fucked up, and I couldn't explain it, but for some reason Touché made me feel like I still had a part of Tino with me. And even though my sister had warned me to stay away from him, I just couldn't bring myself to do that. Because truthfully, I wanted to be around him.

Twenty minutes later, I arrived at a single-family house out in Camp Creek, near the airport. As soon as I pulled into his driveway, I noticed the front door open. Touché was obviously awaiting my arrival.

After parking and turning off the car, I climbed out and approached the house. It was a beautiful, ranch-style bungalow with manicured bushes and shrubbery surrounding it. In the front lawn, I noticed a few dog toys lying around.

"You've got a dog?" I asked before entering his home. I'd never been an advocate of pets, but I particularly hated dogs. They were noisy, irritating, and always slobbering every fucking where.

"Had one. But got rid of it."

After making sure it was safe, I walked inside his house and was surprised by the lavish décor. Almost everything was white; the furniture, the expensive-looking sheepskin rug. I could tell he hired an interior decorator. Either that, or he had some good ass tastes.

Maybe he got a bitch, I thought to myself.

"So what'chu wanna talk about?" Touché asked, interrupting my thoughts.

I turned around and looked at him—and strangely, I saw Tino. Without thinking, I leaned in and crushed my lips against his in hunger and desperation. Touché eagerly rolled with the punches, disregarding the fact that I was his dead homie's girl.

Kicking the door closed behind him, he lifted me up and carried me to the closest couch. My legs were wrapped tight around his waist as we indulged in nasty, sloppy kisses. And although I knew what we were doing was wrong, I had absolutely no intentions of turning back now.

Placing me down on the couch, he roughly yanked my legging down and slipped his hand in my panties. An accidental moan escaped from within me as I enjoyed the magic he created with his fingers. His touch was delicate; he knew just how to stroke my clit.

Reaching for his erection, I was surprised at the massive size and girth he was working with. Homeboy was packing.

Grabbing my other hand, he guided it towards his lips and placed soft, passionate kisses on each of my fingers. "Damn, Kylie," he said, staring into my glassy eyes. "I want'chu in the worst fucking way."

"Then have me, baby..." My words came out hoarse as I savored the satisfaction he was giving me. He had me so wet from playing with my pussy that the couch was soaked. When he slipped two fingers in, I whimpered in pleasure, loving the way he touched me.

"*Mmm.*" He placed fervent kisses along my neck before sucking on my earlobe. "This shit so warm and wet—just like I knew it'd be." He gently eased my panties down my legs. "Lemme see if it tastes how I imagined."

Regret and consequences were the last thing on my mind as I watched him lower himself at waist level and devoured me. "Oh my God! Tino!" I cried out.

Touché was sucking my pussy so good that I couldn't even think straight and accidentally called him his boy's name. I felt him tense up a little but he didn't stop or slow down his effort at making me cum.

"Damn, baby, that feels so good. Yeah, just like that."

Grabbing hold of my thighs, Touché licked faster and harder. You would've thought he was trying to suck the misery out of me. No man had ever eaten my pussy with such a vigorous desire.

"I want you inside me!" I moaned. I could no longer hold off. The teasing was becoming torturous. I needed him; every inch of him.

We were in such a frenzy to undress each other that we both tumbled onto the living room floor. Touché landed on top of me but not hard enough to crush me. He hungrily pressed his lips against mine as he rushed to free his anaconda from its dwelling.

"How do you want me?" I asked in between kisses.

Without answering, he turned me over so that I was on my stomach. Touché flashed a sexy smile as he admired the beautiful view of my plump, beige ass. He gave it a gentle slap and I yelped in delight.

Right when I expected him to put in, he bent down and started eating my pussy from the back. If I didn't know any better, I'd think he was trying to outdo my past lovers. Satisfying each other became a competition. That's how hard he was going. Grinding my ass against my face, I relished the way his soft lips sucked on my juicy clit. He was making me feel so good that suddenly I felt the urge to do the same for him.

I was just about to return the favor when Touché forced me down and entered me from behind. *"Unnnhhh!"* I moaned at his powerful penetration. He didn't even take his time; he wanted me to have every inch he had to give.

"You like that dick? You like how I fill you up?"

"God, yes!" I screamed.

Touché started hitting it fast and hard, his balls slapping my pussy with every stroke. He was digging into me with such force, you would've thought he was about to climb inside.

"Damn. I'mma try to hold out but this shit so good," he said. Grabbing my arm, he gently pinned it behind my back to keep me from running. "Yeah...Keep that ass just like that. Don't you fucking move," he said, pounding into me. "Where you want me to cum?"

"Unh-ahh...Where ever you want, baby," I said seductively.

I assumed hearing me say that must've turned him on, because I felt his dick get harder inside me. He was so big and so solid, that it felt like I was fucking a steel bat. "Damn, this dick good, baby."

"This yo' dick, K. You can have this shit whenever you want it."

The way the words tumbled off his tongue made me wetter. "*Oooh*, I feel myself 'bout to cum."

"Let go, baby. Cum all over this big dick." Touché began playing with my clit in an effort to assist me with the task.

Before I knew it, I was cumming and squirting everywhere.

Touché didn't stop the punishment he was inflicting. He continued to pound me until I came a second and third time. In the distance, I noticed the sun had rose. It felt like we'd been fucking forever, and to be honest, I had no issue if we did.

As we fucked on the living room floor, it felt like we were the only two people on Earth. Like none of our problems existed.

Taking charge, I pushed him off and climbed on top in a reverse cowgirl position. Touché groaned as I eased onto his pole. I could tell he loved the views of my back shots. Sliding up and down his length in slow motion, my pussy struggled to adjust to his girthy size. Touché had one of the biggest dicks I'd ever experienced, and handling him was no easy task.

Grabbing my hips, Touché assisted me with my movements. Up and down. Back and forth. Circular motions. I rode his horse-sized dick like we were at the Kentucky Derby. After letting me take control for several minutes, Touché decided that he wanted to be in charge again.

In one swift movement, he flipped me over and eased between my thighs missionary-style. Gripping my throat, he attacked my pussy with such force he gave me carpet burns. My fingernails dug into his back as I screamed from both pleasure and pain. Touché was killing my shit. You would've thought he was trying to put a baby up in me. He had me gushing my juices all over his dick. That's how wet I was.

"Oh shit!" I cried out.

"Nah. Don't run, bitch. Take this dick," he ordered, slamming into my pelvis repeatedly. "Damn. Here it come."

That time, we came together. My walls tightened around his dick as I shivered and quaked from the powerful orgasm that shook my senses. It was one of the best orgasms I'd ever had in my life.

Touché slowly pulled his dick out and it wasn't until then that I realized he'd came inside of me. "Oh my God. We should've worn a condom."

Little did I know, I had much bigger problems.

The same lust that landed me here would eventually lead me down a dark and dangerous path of self-destruction.

12
CUE

Everyone falls in love sometimes...

I don't know 'bout you but it ain't a crime...

That morning, I was awakened by the music of Tory Lanez and the heavenly scent of breakfast. It felt good to not be opening my eyes in a jail cell. Because of my father's prolific run as a renowned lawyer who worked for all the famous celebrities, I had the best legal team on my defense. They were able to pull a few strings and make sure the charges didn't stick. After all, there was no real evidence against me other than someone else's word—and that simply wasn't enough in my case. Aubrey's plan to see me fall had failed miserably.

I couldn't wait to personally put a bullet in that nigga's head for all the trouble he'd caused thus far. He was a problem that needed to be handled ASAP. But for now, I would enjoy the peace that Khari gave me.

Climbing out the bed, I padded through the house until I located her in the kitchen dancing over the stove. She was cooking in nothing but her bra and panties. Khari was so mothafucking sexy and thick that she made my dick hard just staring at her.

"Mornin', beautiful."

Khari turned around and blushed after I'd caught her dancing.

"Oh please, don't stop on my account."

Khari laughed and did a playful little twerk in her pink boy shorts. Walking up behind her, I wrapped my hands around her waist and buried my face in her natural curls. She had it piled high on top of her head in a messy bun.

I loved that she didn't wear weave or perm her hair. It was refreshing to see a young woman embrace her natural, God-given beauty. Running my hands down her shapely figure, I admired her curves, the arch in her back, and the two dimples right above her ass. Everything about Khari was perfect—even her imperfections.

"How'd you sleep, handsome?" she asked.

"Great since I was next to you."

I was so grateful that she didn't turn her back on me after finding out the truth. For months, I'd deluded myself into thinking she'd leave once she found out I was a kingpin. That fear alone convinced me to hide the truth, even though deep down I knew she deserved it. Now that she knew, I was relieved we were on the same page.

"What'chu in here making?" I asked her.

"Eggs, bacon, blueberry pancakes, and hash."

"Damn. Fuck it up then." She was the only woman who cooked food that rivaled my mom's.

Khari giggled and kissed my cheek.

"I'mma go pick up Ali. Then I gotta head to the airport. I have some business to handle in New York."

Khari frowned in disappointment, but didn't dare dispute it. Being Aubrey's girl for so many years, she understood what came with this street shit. I had millions of dollars sewed up in investments, stocks, and organizations—most of which were located in my hometown.

"When will you be back?" she asked.

"Few days." I slapped her ass. "Don't worry. I'mma be back soon to handle this."

I headed out the kitchen to get dressed but Khari quickly stopped me. "Wait. I gotta question."

"I probably gotta answer."

Khari gave me a serious look. "What are we gonna do about Aubrey?"

"Don't worry. I'mma handle that too."

13

KHARI

The moment Cue left out to get Ali, I chastised myself for not telling him that I was pregnant. Honestly, I was unsure if having another baby was a smart idea. Cue lived such a dangerous lifestyle—one that had almost gotten our son killed. Was it really safe to add another child to the equation?

I was so deep in thought that I didn't immediately hear my phone ringing in the other room. Turning the stove off, I headed to the bedroom and grabbed my iPhone off the nightstand. As soon as I saw Aubrey's name flashing across the screen, I rolled my eyes in utter disgust.

This bum ass bitch gotta lot of nerve calling me.

I thought about sending him straight to voicemail, but I was curious to hear what he had to say. "What the fuck do you want?" I asked with an attitude.

"That's how you answer the phone?"

"No. Just for the mothafuckas who almost get my kid taken."

"You still on that bullshit?"

"How the fuck is my son getting shot in the

chest and spending weeks in the hospital bullshit? If it wasn't for Cue, I would've never gotten him back—"

"Man, fuck Cue. Speaking of that bitch made nigga, I heard he got out." Aubrey gave a low, sinister laugh. "Fool ass nigga don't 'een know he was prolly safer behind bars. But it's cool. He won't be around much longer...so enjoy it while it lasts."

Now it was my turn to laugh. "Cue ain't worried about you, Aubrey. And neither am I."

"Oh yeah?"

"Yep."

Aubrey chuckled. "Glad you seem to find some amusement out this situation. We'll see how funny shit is when you identifying his body parts."

His chilling threat didn't leave me the least bit nervous. "I doubt that'll happen," I told him. "Cue's a big boy. He's more than capable of taking care of himself—and me and Ali," I added for the hell of it.

"Oh, is that right?" I heard the jealousy all in his tone as he said it. "So you think it's cute having that bitch around my son, huh?"

"Yep."

"You a stupid ass bitch!"

I tossed all the cards on the table when I suddenly blurted out, "And Ali ain't your son, nigga! So you tell me who the stupid ass *really* is!"

There was a long, drawn out pause after the truth was finally revealed.

"Bitch! Shut yuh raasclaat mouth!" he yelled. "Yuh no say no shit yuh can't take back. Yuh hear me?"

"Bitch, the only thing I would take back is the eight years I wasted on your ass!"

"Khari, I swear to God. If you telling me the truth, you just killed yo' self! You hear me, bitch? You just killed yo' fucking self!"

"I ain't worried about you or them weak ass threats. My nigga out and I know we gon' be good. So you do what you gotta do, but just know Cue will too."

"I hope it was worth it, cunt!"

"It certainly was. Now I got shit to do so goodbye, Aubrey."

"Khari, don't you fucking hang up this phone—"

"You'll never see me or Ali again. You can believe that shit." And with that, I disconnected the call, having no regards to how the truth may've affected him.

Aubrey could rot in hell for all I cared.

14

AUBREY

Staring at my phone in bewilderment, I asked myself if Khari had said what I think she said. What the fuck did she mean Ali wasn't mine? How could she even let something like that come out her fucking mouth?

I wanted to believe she was talking out of anger, but I knew that Khari wasn't even that type of bitch. She ain't just say shit for the fuck of it. She'd never been one to stoop low only to get a rise out of me.

She gotta be lying though, I convinced myself. However, deep down inside, I knew that it was a strong possibility. Ali and I had never taken a blood test, and there were times when I doubted our resemblance. But I trusted my bitch. She never gave me any reason not to—until today.

"How the fuck could she keep some shit like that from me for almost ten years?!"

Suddenly, I realized that Khari might've been more fucked up than me. I had done a lot of shit in my years, but what she did to me, I would never do to anyone.

Tears filled my eyes as I thought about the greatest memories I'd shared with Ali. I was there when she gave birth. I was right by her side when he said his first words, which were daddy. I was there when he took his first steps, when he threw his first football. How the fuck could Khari lie to me for all those years?

I felt robbed. Like the last decade of my life was a lie. I may not have been Father of the Year, but I loved that lil' boy enough to give my life for if need be. Knowing that he wasn't mine cut deep. It was a pain I'd never experienced; a pain I never prepared for—or expected Khari to inflict. She hurt me so fucking bad.

In a sudden fit of rage, I started trashing my crib. Because it was out in the middle of nowhere, I didn't have to worry about neighbors hearing and calling the cops. A few weeks back, I'd bought a foreclosed baby mansion in hopes that Khari would eventually come to her senses and move back with me. But after the bomb she dropped on me today, that shit would never happen. I planned on burying that bitch right alongside the nigga she pledged her allegiance to.

Overwhelmed by emotions, I dropped to the floor and broke down crying. I had my lil' man tatted on me and everything. I was just that proud of him—handicap and all. He was my everything. The best part of my life. I was beyond distraught. Hell, I was crushed. I didn't even feel like a man anymore.

Wiping my tears, I stood to my feet and walked to the coffee table. Slicing open a brick, I snorted enough coke to OD. I needed something to numb the pain.

Afterwards, I grabbed my phone and hit up my killer. My hands were trembling so bad that I barely could dial his number.

Them bitches can't get handled fast enough.

I wouldn't sleep peacefully until Khari and Cue were body bagged and put in the mothafucking dirt.

15

TOUCHÉ

That morning, I rolled over to the satisfying sight of Kylie in my bed. She was breathtaking when she was asleep. She looked peaceful, beautiful.

Damn.

A feeling of guilt suddenly washed over me after realizing how hurt she'd be if she knew I killed Tino. Kylie had no idea that she was lying with the enemy. And as foul as it was, I had no intentions of telling her, because the truth was, I could see myself fucking with her heavy. And I didn't wanna do shit that might jeopardize that.

Kylie must've felt me watching her, because she slowly cracked her eyes open. Before I could even speak, she snatched the sheets off and quickly sat up in bed. "Oh my God. I didn't mean to spend the night."

I chuckled. "Man, you cool. Chill." I tried to pull her back in bed with me but she pulled away and jumped out the bed.

"Nah. I can't chill. Matter fact, I gotta."

"Damn. Wassup?"

"Wassup is this shit shouldn't have happened. I mean shit, you're Tino's boy. We should've never let things escalate to this point."

"So you having regrets now?" I asked her.

"I regret putting my emotions before common sense," she said, quickly dressing.

"Kylie...come here." I patted the empty space on the bed next to me.

Kylie looked at it, and for a split second I thought she would climb in bed. But instead, she fled my crib without so much as a goodbye.

Damn.

My thoughts were suddenly interrupted by my phone ringing. When I looked at the caller ID, I saw that it was Aubrey—which meant he probably had a lick for me. "Wus good, boss man?"

"I got some shit I need handled," he said.

"Don't worry. I got eyes and ears on that nigga, Cue—"

"Nah, it's more to it than just that," he said. "I need you to put a bullet in that bitch Khari head too. Think you can do that for me?"

"For the right price, I'll put a bullet in any body's head."

I meant that shit too. She might've been Kylie's sister, but a check was a check.

"My nigga. I'mma shoot you a lil' somethin' now for ya troubles. And I'll wire the rest once it's done."

"Cool. Cool," I said rubbing my hands together.

I was picturing all the shit I would do with the money, like renovating the club me and Tino used to own. I'd also had my eye on a Porsche 911 for some time now.

"I can do that for you. But uh...can I ask a quick question?"

I was somewhat curious to know why he wanted his baby mama dead. Even for a cutthroat nigga like him, killing his girl was an all-time low.

"What happened between ya'll, bruh?"

"NONE OF YO' FUCKING COCK-SUCKING BUSINESS, NIGGA! That's what happened!"

"Damn. My bad, G. Sorry for asking, man, chill—"

"Nah, I'mma chill once that bitch and that nigga dead. You feel me?"

"Yeah...I feel you. But what'chu want me to do with the kid though."

There was a long pause on Aubrey's end before he replied, "Kill him."

16

KYLIE

Once I got back to the crib, I showered, washed my hair, and tried my best to forget the fact that I fucked my dead ex's homeboy. What type of bitch did some crazy shit like that? Tino wasn't in the ground a whole month yet, and he was probably rolling over in his grave after witnessing the betrayal.

I was so disgusted with myself that I couldn't even stand the sight of myself. What we did was wrong, and even worse, we couldn't take it back.

"Lil' girl, why are you walking around looking like that?" Mama asked. I was on my way to the bedroom when she stopped me in the hall. She always knew when something was bothering me.

"It's nothing," I lied. I didn't tell her about Tino's death because I didn't want a lecture, and honestly I had no intentions to. I wasn't in the mood for any I-told-you-so's.

Mama gave me a skeptical look. "Okie dokie then. Just know I'm here if you wanna talk." She then disappeared inside her bedroom.

I was about to walk inside mine when the doorbell rang. Since I was closest to the front of the house, I decided to answer. "Don't worry, ma.

I got it!" I called out.

Padding barefoot to the door, I stood on my tip toes and peered through the peephole. Much to my dismay, Touché was standing on the opposite. *Damn.* Can't this nigga take a fucking hint, I asked myself.

Swinging the door open with an attitude, I looked at him like he'd lost his damn mind. He must have to be popping up uninvited.

Ignoring my hostility, he walked right in like he had a personal invite.

"Um...what the fuck are you doing?" I asked him.

Touché shot me a look like I was crazy for coming at him so aggressively. "Hold up, ma. Maybe I need to leave out and come back in again," he said. "We gon' start this shit over."

After stepping outside, he walked back into the home expecting a different, friendlier greeting. Unfortunately for him, he wouldn't get it. "Enough of the games, Touché. Why you here?"

He pulled me towards him. "Why you think?"

I quickly pushed him away. "Touché...you really shouldn't have came," I said, shaking my head. "My sister already said she don't want you here."

"Well, good thing I'm here for you and not ya sister."

"I need privacy."

"No. You need company." Grabbing me by the nape of my neck, he pulled me close again and kissed me.

Tugging on my baby blue sweatshirts, Touché tried to have his way with me right there in the foyer. "T, we can't," I whispered as he kissed my neck. "My mother's home—she's in the other room."

"She won't know what's going on if she don't hear us."

"Touché—"

"Where's your room?"

I knew what the logical thing to do was, but for some reason my body just wasn't in accordance. "Down the hall to the left," I breathed.

Picking me up, he carried me to my bedroom. Once inside, he roughly tossed me on the mattress and started stripping me of my clothes. He then climbed between my thighs and eagerly crushed his lips against mine.

Massaging his rock hard dick through his jeans, I anticipated him putting it in. Touché had that dope dick; one that could potentially turn me into an addict. I was feening for another orgasm. I need him. I needed him so much more than I'd let on.

Fumbling to unbutton his jeans, I snatched them just inches below his waist. His big, black

Mandingo stood at full attention as it oozed of pre-cum.

Foreplay was not needed or missed, as I grabbed his dick and gently eased it inside me. He was a little too much for my tight pussy hole, but I welcomed the combination of pleasure and pain.

"Fuck me, T," I moaned. "Fuck the shit outta me."

Touché slid his fat dick inside me inch by inch, slowly filling me up. I gasped and whimpered as I tried to match his powerful thrusts with my own. I was close to cumming when he pulled out and slapped his big, heavy dick against my clit. My cream painted the flesh of his skin.

Just when I expected him to put it back in, I was instead greeted by the warm sensation of his long, wet tongue Touché buried his face deep in my pussy, licking and lapping like a starved animal.

"*Oohh.* That feels so good," I moaned. Just when I thought I couldn't get enough, he jammed his dick inside me and really gave me something to whimper about.

Naturally, I inched away.

"You wanted it right?" he asked. "Why you running?" Touché grabbed a handful of my hair and pulled gently. "Don't run," he demanded. "Take this dick."

I gripped the sheets as he slammed his dick into me with such force the bed shook. Touché grabbed my right leg and lifted it over his shoulder so that he could dig even further. You would've thought he was trying to put a baby up in me.

"We keep fuckin' like this, you gon' end up mine."

17
CUE

Staring out the wall of windows in my penthouse condo, I admired the New York City skyline while sipping a glass of cognac. Nas' *"Stillmatic"* poured through the built-in Bluetooth speakers as I thought about a future with Khari. She was the female version of me; my other half, and I couldn't envision a life without her. She was my everything and I would do whatever it took to ensure her and Ali's safety.

Even though she was in Atlanta, I made sure to have a couple killers keeping watch. With Aubrey lurking around, I had to play it safe. I didn't want a repeat of what happened last time. I'd foolishly let myself think that I was invincible, but I would never make that mistake. And I would never allow anything to happen to my loved ones.

Looking down at the black velvet box in my hand, I made a silent promise to protect them with my life. Lifting the lid to the jewelry box, I stared at the engagement ring I planned on giving Khari.

Now that I knew Ali was for sure mine, I wanted to make this shit official. I was ready for her to be Mrs. Saldana.

Since Khari was so heavy on my mind, I decided to reach out to her. I'd be in New York for a few days, so the least I could do was check on her and see how she was doing. Khari answered her phone on the third ring.

"You missing me already?" she asked. I could hear her smiling through the phone.

"How could I not?"

"How's New York? Is it warm up there?"

"Eh. Lil' chilly. Honestly, I can't wait to get back to Georgia. I've really gotten acclimated to the weather."

"I've really got acclimated to you," she teased.

Her comment was enough to elicit a laugh. "I've got a surprise for you when I get back."

"*Mmm*. I can't wait." She assumed I was talking about sex, but she had no idea I had something much more powerful and meaningful in store.

"How's lil' man?" I asked her.

"He's good. I had to get in his ass earlier about cleaning up after himself, but you know that's nothing new."

"And your mom? How's she doing?"

Khari's mother was recently involved in a near fatal car accident. She'd only been out of the hospital a month or so.

"She's doing wonderful. Walking on her own finally and healing rather quickly."

"That's good to hear."

Khari paused. "Cue...before we hang up, there's something I wanna talk to you about."

"Wassup, bay?"

"Shane...he murdered my cousin," she said. "I wanted to know if you could—"

"It's already been handled."

There was a long pause on Khari's end. She didn't expect to hear me say that, and I didn't expect her to ask. After all, I tried to keep my personal life separate from my business life.

Starr and I may have had our differences, but I'd be damned if I let the nigga live that killed her. I had the mothafucka brutally murdered a week after her funeral, and his body tossed in a river three hours from the city. Unlike Starr, he didn't deserve a proper burial.

"And how did you handle it?" she pressed.

"The details aren't important Khari. Just know it's handled."

"The details aren't important...or you don't wanna give me the details?"

"That'd be preferable," I answered truthfully.

All of a sudden, there was a knock on my door. "I gotta go. I'll hit you later, aight. Answer."

"Okay. I love you, Cue."

"I love you more, Khari."

After disconnecting the call, I pocketed my phone and placed the engagement ring on the mantle. When I finally answered the door, I saw the very last person I expected to see.

18
CUE

Standing before me was my estranged ex-girlfriend, Jennifer—looking damn good in a pair of asshole tight skinny jeans and crop top. Her ripe cleavage was on full display, showcasing the tat of my name near her collarbone.

I wouldn't have been surprised if she put the most form-fitting outfit on she could find before coming over. Jennifer loved to lure me back in using her exotic beauty and sexuality.

Born to a black mother and Nicaraguan father, Jennifer had smooth bronze skin, piercing hazel eyes, and long, jet black silky hair that reached her ass. Speaking of ass, that mothafucka was sitting up rather nicely.

My dick sprang to life at the thought of spreading them apart.

I loved the fuck out of my girl, and I couldn't live without her, but the aspect of stabbing at something different seemed inviting…

I quickly shook the lustful thoughts from my mind after remembering all the bullshit Jennifer put me through. "What the fuck is you doing here?"

Jennifer smiled. "Oh, so you ain't happy to see me?" she asked. "'Cuz the bulge in your pants says otherwise."

My cheeks flushed in embarrassment, and all I could think to say was, "You got two seconds to answer, or you gon' be talking to the door."

Jennifer took a bold step towards me and grabbed my dick. "How 'bout we do something more interesting than talk?"

Backing me into my apartment, she quickly began to unbutton my pants. There was an internal battle that I struggled with as I watched her work. She had me hard than a mothafucka, and I wanted her like crazy—but I wasn't trying to go down that road again.

Grabbing her hands, I stopped her from pulling my dick out and exposing how much I desired her. "Stop. We ain't finna do that."

Jennifer looked up at me and pouted in disappointment. "Why not?"

"Why the fuck you think? 'Cuz you cheated on me. It's over between us."

"You cheated on me too, Cue, but hey, who's keeping score?"

After leaving Atlanta—and Starr—five years ago, I moved back home to New York, and met Jennifer, an up and coming model, who waitressed part time at a diner in midtown. In the beginning, everything was perfect—but shit always started off that way.

Over time, her true colors began to surface. Jennifer was a sneaky, money hungry, spoiled bitch that stressed me to the point of getting gray hairs. Now that she was out of my life, I didn't plan on ever opening that chapter again.

As beautiful as she was, I just couldn't be with someone who took and took and never had anything to give in return. Jennifer had no real aspirations in life other than being a rich nigga's trophy wife. I didn't need a girl like that. I needed a woman like Khari.

Jennifer reached for my dick again but I quickly stopped her. Had it not been for my strong will, I would've already bent her thick ass over. But I knew the second I nutted, I would regret the shit.

"Look, I told you to fucking chill," I said, grabbing her by the throat.

"How can I chill when I've been missing you like crazy?" she asked. "One of the worst feelings is to be single but mentally taken. I think about you every day. I know it's been over between us for a while, but I can't get you off my mind. I miss you, Cue. I miss everything about you—especially this dick." She rubbed my erection while licking her lips seductively. She was really pulling all the stops just to get some dick.

"So this what the fuck you came over here for?" I laughed. "Bitch, you lost that privilege. Or did you forget?"

Jennifer smiled. "Actually...I came here for

this..."

Suddenly, and without warning, she jammed her pistol in my stomach and pulled the trigger.

POP!

19
CUE

Stumbling backwards, I clutched my stomach in an attempt to stop the bleeding. I couldn't fucking believe this crazy ass bitch had shot me! Blood soaked my shirt and poured through my fingers, painting the marble floors of my condo. I looked at the gun in her hand with the suppressor screwed on the end. She had me so riled up, I didn't even notice she was packing.

"What the fuck, J?" My voice strained because of the pain I was in. Both physical and emotion. This was something I didn't foresee. "Why would you do this?"

"Why do you think, asshole? Because of the money! It's always been about the money!"

Backing away in terror, I tried to reason with her. "How much is he paying you?"

"Enough to be set for a *looooonng* time, mothafucka" she boasted.

"Take me to the hospital. I'll give you double—"

"Fuck you and your money, Cue!" she spat. "You don't fucking get it, do you? It's too late to try and win me over! You made your choice when you chose Atlanta and that fat ass bitch over me! Now it's my turn to make my choice!"

"You don't wanna do this," I told her.

Jennifer smiled sadistically. "You're wrong," she said. "...I've never wanted to do anything more." She squeezed the trigger.

POP!

I quickly ducked and ran towards my bedroom to retrieve my gun, making sure to keep my head down.

POP!

POP!

POP!

POP!

Jennifer continued to let off rounds, shattering a lamp, vase, and a floor-to-ceiling window in the living room. One of the bullets struck me in the back of my shoulder, but luckily I was able to make it to my junk drawer.

Fumbling with grabbing my gun, I rushed to slide a magazine inside. I'd just locked the slide when Jennifer appeared in the doorway with her gun aimed at me. There was a sadistic look in her eyes that almost made her unrecognizable. I couldn't believe this was a woman I'd once loved. I almost didn't know who the fuck she was. The Jennifer that I fell for would've never pulled this shit.

Greed could be so destructive.

"Don't make me do this," I told her. My

body was growing weaker and weaker by the second. I needed a hospital and bad or else I would bleed to death.

"How could you walk away from me like that? I loved you!"

"You loved what I could do for you—"

"That's bullshit and you know it! You meant everything to me and you just shitted all over my heart!" she yelled. "I bet you didn't even know I was pregnant at the time we broke up, did you?" Tears poured down her cheeks. "I lost the baby. I lost my job. I lost everything! Don't you get it? I *have* to do this," she cried. "I have to—"

"You don't have to."

"I loved you, Cue and you just left! That seems to be a habit of yours. You walked out on Starr. You walked out on me. I guess it's safe to say this new bitch would've been next. I guess, in a way, I'm doing her a favor." Jennifer pointed her gun at me—

POP!

POP!

POP!

POP!

POP!

POP!

POP!

I unloaded my clip into her before she even had the chance to squeeze.

Jennifer stumbled backwards towards the shattered window before falling through and plummeting 32 stories.

The gun slipped from my fingers and dropped to the floor as I began to feel lightheaded. All of a sudden, everything went black and I collapsed from blood loss.

20

AUBREY

Migos' *"I'd Rather Be Rich Than Famous"* poured through the speakers in my 'bando as me and a bunch of GD niggas bust down a new shipment of product. I'd kept all my prison connects, ensuring them a secure position with my empire for years to come.

I had a new Mexican plug that sent me the bricks across the water on freighters. The product was pure, un-stepped on and rivaled all of my competitors. What I used to sell for 35, I now sold for 28 in order to wipe out the competition. Cue's buyers would slowly gravitate to me because of the awesome deal they were getting.

Success was the sweetest revenge.

I smiled at the thought of Cue lying on a cold, metal slab in the morgue. If he wasn't already on his way there now, it'd only be a matter of time.

Touché wasn't the only one I had hired to kill him. I'd employed multiple people with the task, in hopes that the job would be handled faster. My pops always told me *'having one option is not an option'*. Therefore, I had all types of mothafuckas on my payroll, looking to put him in the ground—including his ex-girlfriend, Jennifer.

Now that nigga gon' see how it feels to be

down and out.

Cue had left me for dead in the Feds, turned Carmine against me, and stole my family. I was past due for some much deserved payback. Cue had taken everything from me that I loved. And in the end, it was only fair that I take it all back.

Karma was a mothafucka.

I was feeling real good about shit. Things were looking up, money was in rotation, and soon there would be no one standing in my way of reaching the top.

Suddenly, my phone started ringing, interrupting my thoughts. I was hoping that it was Jennifer, calling to give me the good news. But as soon as I saw the number on the screen, I knew the only news I'd be getting was bad news.

When I answered the phone, Cue's deep voice filled the receiver. He sounded weak and mentally drained, but alive nonetheless. "To kill me, you gon' have to try harder, mothafucka."

21

TOUCHÉ

That afternoon, I met with contractors to discuss renovations for the club Tino and I co-owned. The shoot-out had left the place in shambles, so it needed a complete overhaul and marketing strategy to once again be successful. I had too much money sewed up in the place to just walk away from it. I had no choice but to restore it if I didn't want negative equity.

After the meeting ended, I decided to swing by Kylie's crib to check up on her. She hated whenever I popped up on her unannounced, but I figured we were well past that by now. Hell, she'd already let me smash twice without a hat. There was no sense in her even making an issue about the shit, when she was as good as mine.

Pushing my copper toned McLaren P1, I headed to her side of town with hopes that she'd let me hit again. I was slowly turning into an addict for Kylie, whether she knew it or not.

Bending the corner to the block she lived on, I pulled up to her crib and noticed that she was talking to some nigga in the driveway. After recognizing who he was, I was overcome by a sudden surge of resentment. Kylie wasn't my girl but I damn sure ain't wanna see her with some clown ass nigga.

Fuming with rage, my grip on the steering

wheel tightened. *She don't wanna see a young nigga's bad side,* I told myself. Kylie had me hot than a mothafucka. She ain't know I was the jealous type but she would soon find out.

If it weren't for the fact that it was broad daylight, I would've blew that nigga's head off his mothafucking shoulders. I was just that heated.

Shit, I still owed him one after coming to my club on that bullshit a few months back. At the time, Tino had promised that he would take care of it, but now that he was gone, the task was left up to me.

Instead of handling the situation right then, I chose to keep driving. Jamaal would get his issue *real* soon.

Enjoy it while it lasts mothafucka...

22

TOUCHÉ

Bumping my Migos mixtape, I drove through east Atlanta in search of Jamaal. After asking around, I found out that he usually hung out in the hood with a bunch of niggas that were known jack boys.

This bitch sure knows how to pick 'em, I thought to myself.

With my double barrel pump action shotgun under my seat, I was ready to take a nigga's head—and it was looking like Jamaal would be my next victim.

Had it not been for me running into him today, I would've forgotten all about the beef he had with my boy Tino. Because he was still sniffing around Kylie, he now had beef with me. And niggas that I beefed with ain't live to tell the story.

Pulling up to a hole in the wall bar called Tommy's, I killed the engine to my McLaren and hopped out with murderous intentions. I decided to leave the shottie in the car, and instead opted for a Ruger .357 Magnum.

Posted up in front of the spot were a couple young bulls, mean-mugging the fuck out of me as I approached them. They were probably trying to figure out who the hell I was, and why the fuck I was on their turf.

"Wus good?" the apparent leader asked me. He was a tall, burly mothafucka that reminded me of the nigga who played BIG in the movie, *Notorious*. "You *need* something?"

I assumed he was referring to drugs, but what I required could not be fulfilled by a temporary high. I wanted Jamaal's head—and balls—on a silver mothafucking platter. Fuck some narcotics.

"Yeah, I *do* need something. You know where I can find the nigga, Jamaal?" I asked him.

My question made him step in my face with an attitude. "Who the fuck wanna know, nigga?"

BLOW!

I put a fucking bullet through his head the second he got out of line. I ain't have time for arrogant mothafuckas who thought this shit was a game. I was on a mothafucking warpath, and anybody that got in my way could get put down too.

When his niggas reached for their guns, I quickly pointed mine at them. "I wouldn't do that—unless you wanna end up on the ground with this pussy ass nigga."

They looked down at their boy's dead body, and the smoke that was coming out the tiny hole in his head.

"Now we gon' try this shit again," I said. "Where the fuck that nigga, Jamaal at?"

The youngest quickly spoke up before I made another example out of them. "He—he inside!" he answered nervously.

Pushing my way past them, I barged in the bar and looked around for Kylie's ex. The only people in the bar were a couple of lone drunks and a few niggas shooting pool. Nothing out of the ordinary, but not quite what I was hoping for either.

Man, where the fuck is this nigga, I asked myself?

I did a second look through in case I'd missed him the first time. The mothafucka definitely said he was in here.

When I didn't see him, I assumed the nigga outside had lied to me. I was about to go out there and check him when I suddenly felt the cold steel of a gun pressed against the back of my skull.

"You looking for me?" Jamaal asked.

23
TOUCHÉ

"Shit, from where I'm standing, it looks like *you* the one looking for *me*," I told him.

"Turn around, bitch. I want you to look me in the eyes when I pull the mothafucking trigger."

Ever so slowly, I did as I was told.

"I'll take that," he said, relieving me of my weapon.

I grilled the fuck out of Jamaal, hating the mere sight of his ass. This nigga was craftier than I thought, but I was too prideful to openly admit it.

"Before I pull this trigger, I guess I owe it to myself to at least find out why the fuck you were looking for me?"

"Why the fuck was you at Kylie's?" I asked him.

Jamaal shook his head. "Answering a question with a question, aight then. Well, if you must know, I was trying to get that ole thing back. Been chasing this bitch nonstop for months." He chuckled. "Good pussy make a nigga act crazy. You know what I mean?"

I didn't answer. Instead, I just continued to stare daggers at him. Jamaal was fucking with me for the hell of it.

"What am I talking 'bout? Of course you know what I mean. That's why you did all this shit, right? Killed my boy out front? Over some pussy."

I shrugged my shoulders. "Shit, like you said. Good pussy make a nigga act crazy."

Jamaal laughed. "You right," he said, cocking the hammer.

I closed my eyes and prepared to meet my maker.

POP!

The lone gunshot was followed by a soft thud—that didn't come from my own body. When I opened my eyes, I saw Jamaal lying in a puddle of blood with a bullet hole in the back of his head.

Lowering his gun, Aubrey frowned at the splotches of blood on his white Versace shirt. A group of GD niggas were right by his side like he was Pablo Escobar or some shit. "Damn, nigga. You got me out here doing *your* mothafucking job. What the fuck am I paying you for, nigga?" he asked me.

"Man, I had it covered," I lied, knowing damn well I was two seconds away from being murked.

"If that's what'chu call being on the receiving end of a bullet, then yeah. You had shit under control." Aubrey's tone was dripping with sarcasm.

I didn't mind though, because deep down

inside, I was happy than a mothafucka that he came through. If it wasn't for him, I'd be lying right where Jamaal was with a bullet in my brain instead of him.

"How the fuck you know where to find me anyway?" I asked him.

"Nigga, I got the streets on lock now," he bragged. "I know every fucking thing. But what I can't seem to figure out is why Cue and Khari are still alive...since you *so-called got shit covered.*"

"I'm still working on it," I told him.

"Well, mothafucka, I'mma need you to work harder."

24

KYLIE

I was painting my toenails with the TV on when news of a tragic shooting at a bar in East Atlanta suddenly caught my attention. The only reason that I noticed was because it was the same place Jamaal liked to hang out at.

He had come by earlier, spitting some weak ass penitentiary game to get me back, but this time I wasn't budging. My life was on the line—all because he'd lied to me. No matter what he did or what he said, I could never forgive him. I could never go back to a nigga like that.

Turning up the volume to my TV, I listened in to see what had happened.

"...Developing story on a shooting at a local bar, where two people were gunned down just hours ago. Unfortunately, there were no cameras inside, and no witnesses have come forward to identity the suspects. The victims are 26-year old Maurice Evans and 25-year old Jamaal Baxter. Now details are still underway and we're asking anyone with information to call Crime Stoppers..."

I quickly clamped a hand over my mouth as tears filled my eyes. I couldn't believe what the fuck I was seeing and hearing. Jamaal was dead?!

My chest tightened and suddenly I felt like I couldn't breathe. I'd just saw him earlier and now he was gone? This shit didn't seem real!

Is this really happening, I asked myself.

Warm tears cascaded down my cheeks; I just couldn't accept the truth. My heart wouldn't allow it. Sure, Jamaal and I had our differences, but I didn't want to see him killed. Pulling my hair, I broke down crying hysterically.

Jamaal and I weren't together, but it felt like I'd lost a part of myself. Hell, he was my first love. The man I'd lost my virginity to—the father of the son we'd lost. I almost couldn't bare what the fuck I was seeing. It was just too much.

I assumed Mama must've heard me weeping because she walked in with a look of concern. "Kylie...what's the matter, baby?" she asked.

I didn't bother answering as I jumped up, grabbed my phone, and left out the house. There was only one person who I knew was capable of doing something this fucked up—and I couldn't wait to check the shit out of him.

***

Two hours later, I found Touché at Tino's favorite lounge shooting pool like he hadn't done a damn thing wrong. He was so focused on not fucking up his shot that he didn't even see me walk in.

As soon as I reached him, I slapped the shit out of him. "It was you, wasn't it?!" I screamed. "I thought I saw you drive past earlier! You saw us! *It was you!*"

Touché snatched me up by my throat. "Bitch, is you out'cho mothafucking mind hitting me?! I should break yo' mothafucking hands—"

"Nah, why don't you do me the way you did Jamaal, you fucking coward!" I hocked up a glob of mucus and spat in his face.

WHAP!

Touché slapped the piss out of me, causing my bottom lip to split.

"You fucking tripping, man! I don't even know what the fuck you talking bout!" he said, wiping his face.

"You killed him!" I yelled with tears in my eyes. "You murdered Jamaal, didn't you?!"

Touché jumped around my question like a professional dodge player. "Man, get the fuck outta here with that bullshit. I don't know what the fuck you on but take that shit elsewhere."

I quickly grabbed one of the balls off the pool table and launched it at his head—but Touché quickly ducked.

The men standing around the pool table looked at us like we were crazy, but no one stepped up to my defense. They obviously didn't want to get involved in something that had nothing to do with them—especially when it involved a crazy ass nigga like Touché.

"Bitch, I kill niggas for doing less! You throw some shit at me again, and that's gon' be the last thing you ever fucking do! You hear me?"

I pushed him. "Fuck you!"

"Fuck you, bitch! Get the fuck outta here!"

"Make me, ho!"

I went to slap him again, but he grabbed my hand, twisted it behind my back and forced me down on the pool table so that my face was pressed against the surface. After realizing what was about to go down, the niggas quickly evacuated the room.

"Get the fuck off me, bitch!" I screamed.

"Nah, you wanna come here on that bullshit? I got something for yo' ass!" he said, unbuttoning his jeans. The niggas were barely out the room before he shoved his dick deep inside me.

"*Unnnhhh!*" I yelped. His penetration was a combination of pleasure and pain.

"This what'chu want, bitch? To get fucked? This why you acting crazy?"

I tried to push him off even though the shit was feeling so good. "You...killed...him," I cried.

Touché sped up his pace as he hit it from the back in an aggressive, doggish manner. "I'mma kill this pussy. That's what the fuck I'mma kill."

"*Unnnhh*—stop," I moaned.

Touché grabbed a handful of my hair. "Bitch, you don't want me to stop. That's why this pussy getting wetter."

I hated him because he was telling the truth. Touché had me dripping juices down my legs, when just moments ago, I was ready to kill him. I would never understand how he had that effect on my body. The lust I felt for him was deadly ...but for some reason, I insisted on playing with fire.

"God, I'm 'bout to cum!" I bellowed.

"Cum all over this dick," he coached. Lifting one leg up on the table, he started hitting it deeper, and at an angle that touched my G-spot. "You my bitch now. You hear me? You my fucking bitch now, Kylie. You belong to me."

25

KHARI

ONE WEEK LATER

After picking Ali up from school, I decided to swing past Mama's place to check on her and Kylie. Since Kylie never answered the phone when I called anymore, I figured it was better if we spoke face-to-face. I'd recently heard about Jamaal getting killed, so I could only imagine the toll his death was taking on her—especially after just losing Tino.

As soon as I pulled up to the house, I noticed Touché leaving out and Kylie standing in the doorway wearing nothing but an oversized t-shirt. *His* t-shirt if I probably had to guess.

Damn. So they fucking around now, I thought to myself, putting two and two together. *That explains why the bitch been MIA.* New dick can make a chick go missing.

I couldn't believe Kylie was dealing with Touché, and after I'd already warned her to stay away from him. It was one thing to disregard my advice, but to have him in and out of our mama's house was a whole other story. It was disrespectful.

She don't know shit about that nigga. And while I didn't know very much about Touché either, I knew enough to know he was trouble.

After parking my car in front of the house, I hopped out with my son and made sure to keep him close to me once again. I didn't miss the opportunity to shoot him a nasty look once we made eye contact.

I wasn't going to hide my obvious disdain for the man. I didn't like him, plain and simple— and I could care less how he interpreted my body language and standoffishness. Touché didn't say shit to me as he headed to his car parked in the driveway.

"Mommy, I want one of those when I'm old enough to drive," Ali said, pointing to his McLaren.

Touché stopped, turned to face Ali, and knelt down in front of him. "You know I said the same thing when I was your age 'bout a similar car."

"And now you got it," Ali said, unaware that he was smiling in the face of the devil.

"That's right. I learned the value of hard work by working hard," he said. "So just know when you grow up, you can have anything you want as long as you hustling—"

"My son will *never* be a hustler!" I spat.

I was ready to stab Touché for even speaking to my son. The nerve of him to try and corrupt a child with materialism.

Touché stood to his feet. "That's too bad,"

he said. "'Cuz I know the lil' nigga got it in him—"

Snatching the loaded pistol out my purse, I shoved the barrel in Touché's face, ready to pull the trigger if he said one more word.

"Chill. I was just fucking with you."

"Khari, what the fuck are you doing?!" Kylie cried from the doorway. She didn't expect me to pull a gun out on her little boyfriend.

"Something I should've *been* done!"

"Khari, put that fucking down before you hurt someone!" Kylie demanded.

"Maybe that's what I wanna do," I told her.

"Be careful now," he said with a devilish grin. "And know that if you pull that trigger, you ain't gon' be able to undo what you've done. Your son grows up without a mommy and he'll end up hustling regardless."

"Fuck you!"

Mama quickly rushed outside after hearing all of the ruckus. "Khari! Khari, what the hell are you doing? Put that gun down, girl, before someone sees you and calls the police—"

"Call them! Let them come so I can tell 'em about how you like to run up in houses and shoot little   kids!"
Mama and Kylie looked confused. "Khari, what are you talking about?" Kylie asked.

"I have no idea," Touché said.

"Khari, put that damn gun down and get in the house!" Mama snapped. "You're scaring Ali!"

When I looked down and saw the frightened look on my son's face, I felt horrible. Avoiding the urge to shoot Touché, I lowered my gun and watched as he pompously walked towards his car.

"It's all good. Nothing personal. We all have bad days," he said.

"Get the fuck out of here before shit *really* gets bad!" I warned him. "And don't bring your ass back!"

"I'll see you around, Kylie," he said, climbing into his car.

It took everything in me not to shoot the fucking windshield out. The second he pulled off, Kylie went in on me.

"Khari, what the fuck is your problem—"

"No, what the fuck is *your* problem?! I specifically told you to stay away from him—"

"Girl, I'm not your fucking child! I don't have to do what the fuck you tell me to!"

"Apparently, you do, 'cuz you don't seem to make the right choices on your own!" I then noticed that her eyes were glassy. She was back on drugs and probably stealing again too. Kylie was so damn predictable.

"Bitch, why the fuck are you so affected by

my choices anyway?! You act like you want the nigga!"

"Yeah, I want him in a fucking casket!" I shot back.

"Girl, Touché didn't do anything to you. You just want a reason not to like him because you hate seeing me happy."

"Oh, please." I waved her off. "Now you're just talking crazy."

"No, I'm talking sane, bitch. It's the truth!" Kylie yelled. "You hate to see me happy 'cuz you miserable as fuck! You so fucking sad and pathetic that you had to go and steal your cousin's man! Now you think you somebody 'cuz you let the nigga put a baby up in you!"

Mama gasped and covered her mouth in shock. "Khari, you're pregnant?"

Kylie was the only person I'd told, because I was still unsure of what to do.

"Mommy, you're having another baby?" Ali asked. He had read his grandmother's lips and knew everything now. The cat was finally out of the bag. There was a look of disappointment on Ali's face since I didn't mention it to him first.

I was so damn hurt that Kylie opened her big mouth, I could've killed her. "That'll be the last time I trust your bitter ass with anything," I told her. "C'mon, Ali. Let's go."

I was about to leave but Kylie jumped off

the porch and ran in my face. "*Bitter*? Really? Bitch, you the last person who should be calling somebody bitter! You been lying about who Ali's father was for the last eight years! All because Cue ain't want your raggedy, fat ass back then. You tell me who the bitter bitch *really* is?!"

WHAP!

I slapped the shit out of Kylie as soon as she let the truth slip from her lips.

"*KHARI!*" Mama yelled, rushing to Kylie's side. "What the hell is wrong with you?! You don't fight family!"

What's she talking about mommy, Ali asked using sign language.

Ignoring his question, I went off on my twin sister. "You know what? You do whatever the fuck you want with that nigga! I'm done trying to look out for you!"

"Good! 'Cuz I don't need you to!"

I shook my head at Kylie in disbelief. I couldn't even stand to look at this ho. "Bitch, you are so dead to me it ain't even funny. I told you that shit in confidence, not to use against me as ammunition! You're supposed to be my sister— my *twin* sister at that! I'm supposed to be able to trust you! I'm supposed to be able to count on you! But it's obvious that I can't because you'll never grow the fuck up!" I yelled. "You're a grown ass woman still living at home with her mama. I don't know who's sorrier between you and that nigga! Hell, ya'll two deserve each other! So you do whatever the hell you want with him—and when he plays your stupid ass, don't come running to me!"

"Don't worry, bitch, I won't," she said. "Matter fact, I never have!"

Grabbing Ali by the hand, I headed towards the car, ignoring Mama's pleas for me to come in the house and talk. I wanted to get as far away from them as possible. I had never felt more humiliated and betrayed in my life.

"Don't be bitter, sis, be better!" Kylie yelled after me.

26

KYLIE

After Khari left, and I calmed down a little, I realized how childish and out of line I truly was. My sister was right. I had no business throwing the truth out there for Mama and Ali to hear. If she wanted them to know, she would tell them on her own accord. It wasn't for me to air her dirty laundry the way that I did, and I felt terrible about it.

What the fuck is wrong with me? Why would I do some shit like that?

Regret was eating me alive. Khari had trusted me with her deepest, darkest secrets and I'd let her down. All because I couldn't control my temper and emotions.

Honestly, the only reason I'd wanted to hurt her was because everything she said about me was true. I was a loose cannon with no regard to my own safety, and my sister had called me out on it. I couldn't handle the truth, so I took an all-time low by putting her on blast.

I didn't care about her son being there, and that was wrong of me. I should've handled the situation better instead of acting petty and immature.

Normally, my twin sister and I got along for the most part. We never fought, and when we did have tiny spats, they were never of this magnitude. However, I had a feeling, Khari would never look at me the same after all this shit. But the truth was, I couldn't even look at myself.

Ever since Tino's death, I had been on a downward spiral to self-destruction. I was losing myself—and those I cared about. *What the fuck is happening to me*, I asked myself. *Who the fuck am I now?*

Khari was right. I had a lot of soul-searching and growing up to do. But first I had to make things right with my twin. She didn't deserve to be treated like shit—especially when she was only looking out for my best interest.

I was dead ass wrong, and I knew that I had to undo the damage I'd caused, before it cost me my relationship with my sister.

27

TOUCHE

Yo Gotti's *"The Art of Hustle"* poured through the subwoofers in my AMG as I rounded the corner Khari lived on. Aubrey was right. It was time to handle that bitch once and for all.

Not only was she a problem for him, she was beginning to be a problem for me too. And I ain't need that shit. It was time for that ho to lay down. *I should've been taken care of this bitch.*

After parking a few houses down, I killed the engine and headlights to my truck. There were two cars parked outside her place that I knew were keeping watch for anything suspicious.

Too bad they weren't watching hard enough.

Reaching in the backseat, I grabbed my aluminum suitcase and popped the lid. Inside was a brand new chopper with a scope and beam. Some high-tech shit I bought from my Russian gun supplier.

After assembling the weapon, I screwed a suppressor on the end, so that no one in the neighborhood heard the gunshots. Them mothafuckas wouldn't know what hit 'em.

Quietly climbing out the truck, I grabbed my chopper and found a good vantage point that was several feet from her crib. Peering through the scope, I noticed two men in one car and one in the other.

PFEW!

PFEW!

My aim was impeccable as I shot and killed the first two niggas in Car #1. After hearing glass shatter, the third jumped out with a pistol in his grip.

PFEW!

I blew a hole through his head before he even had a chance to see me.

I was about to run up in Khari's crib, when the front door suddenly opened, and she walked out. An evil grin spread across my lips because she'd made it that much easier for me.

After I dropped that bitch, I planned on putting a bullet in that lil' nigga's head and collecting my final payment. I had no sympathy about taking the life of a child. In my profession, you couldn't have compassion. That shit would get you killed.

Resting my finger on the trigger, I watched her through the scope as she descended the front steps of her home. Because it was dark, she didn't immediately see the dead body lying on the ground across the street. She more than likely didn't hear the gunshots either. A lack of awareness would cost Khari her life.

PFEW!

A single bullet pierced her back, sending her crashing to the ground. Sadly, she didn't even see the shit coming.

In order to make sure she was dead, I tossed the chopper back in my car and grabbed a loaded 9. Screwing the silencer on, I cautiously made my way over towards her. She was sprawled out on the front lawn.

Khari wasn't moving, and from where I stood, it didn't look like she was breathing either.

POP!

I put another bullet in her chest when I reached her just in case.

The way she jerked after the gunshot let me know she was still very much alive—but barely.

Blood gushed from her wounds and mouth as she choked from internal bleeding. There were tears in her eyes, and I could tell she didn't expect this to happen to her. Hell, I didn't even expect it. I never thought Aubrey would ask me to kill his bitch. But I would put a bullet in just about anybody for the right price—guilty or innocent.

I didn't give a fuck.

Khari struggled to raise her hand in an attempt to keep me from shooting again. She was in so much pain that she was trembling and unable to speak.

I pointed my gun at her head and rested

my finger on the trigger—

"Tou—che..." she struggled to say. "Why...?"

My heart dropped to the pit of my stomach after realizing that I'd accidentally shot Kylie.

"Fuck!" I quickly dropped to her side to survey the damage. The tears in my eyes blinded me and I was overwhelmed with emotions. This shit was not happening. This was not how it was supposed to play out. "Damn, Kylie, what the fuck, man? Why the fuck did you have to be here?" I cried.

She reached up and touched my cheek, smearing her blood across my face. "Was it...you?" she struggled to ask. "Did you...kill...Tino?"

Tears slipped from my eyes and dripped onto her forehead. I wanted so badly to lie to her but I knew she deserved the truth. After what I had just done to her, the least I could do was keep it real. Kylie deserved that much.

Swallowing my pride, I nodded my head in misery.

Tears poured down her cheeks as she stared at me in sadness, confusion, and hatred. She didn't have the strength or will to ask why as her hand slipped from my face. "I'll see you in hell..." she said before taking her final breath.

28

KHARI

After hearing all the noise outside, I opened the door to see what was going on and found my sister lying motionless in a pool of blood. "Oh my God! *NO*! Kylie!" Rushing to her side, I checked her pulse, but was unable to located one.

She was gone.

"Mommy...?"

When I turned around, I saw Ali standing in the doorway with a frightened expression on his face. I had just tucked him into bed but he must've sensed that something was wrong.

"No! Go back in the house!" I told him, not wanting him to see Kylie like this. He was just a child, and I didn't want him mentally scarred more than he already was.

"What's wrong with auntie—"

"You don't need to see this! GO IN THE HOUSE!" I yelled.

Ali ran off crying as I held my sister close to me, cradling her in my arms. The pain that I felt was unbearable. I felt like I was the one who had died.

Kylie came over to apologize to me for the way she acted earlier, and we had made up, laughed and even talked shit—and now she was dead.

This shit felt surreal.

This is not happening!

Why would someone do this to my sister?

I just didn't understand.

Crying hysterically, I held onto her until one of the neighbors pried me loose so that the EMTs could take her away. I was so grief-stricken by her death that I didn't even notice or hear the ambulance and police sirens. Apparently, one of the neighbors had called for help.

Two of the officers had to hold me back to keep me from impeding on the task of putting her onto the stretcher. I wasn't ready to let go of my sister. I needed more time with her. Twenty-five years just wasn't long enough.

***

Cue rushed back to Atlanta after hearing the news and met me and Mama at Emory Hospital. Mama was so distraught by the news that she refused to speak to anyone, including me.

As soon as Cue entered the waiting room, I felt a strange feeling of regret. When I called and told him what happened, I thought that I needed him for support. But now that I was seeing him in person, I hated the very fucking sight of him.

Why the fuck did I call him here, I asked

myself. *This shit is all his fault.*

I thought about how Ali's shooting was tied to him—along with Touché. Anything bad that happened was always somehow connected to him.

"Khari...I tried to get here as fast as I could," he said, rushing to me.

WHAP!

Out of nowhere, I hauled off and slapped the shit out of him, having no regard that his arm was in a sling. I simply wanted to hurt him the same way that I was hurting inside. For God's sake, I'd lost my sister.

"Just go!" I screamed at him. "I don't even know why I called you here! I don't wanna look at you!"

Usually, Mama rushed to my side to calm me down, but this time she stayed out of it. She was in a world of her own as she sat with a spaced out look on her face, still in disbelief about her daughter's death.

"Khari, I—"

"Just shut the fuck up, Cue! I don't wanna hear it! Everything always comes back to you! If we'd never started fucking around, Kylie and Starr would still be alive! Everything is your fucking fault! I hate you! I wish I never fell in love with you!"

Cue looked hurt by my accusations, but

stood his ground nonetheless. "You want someone to blame, that's fine. Blame me. But don't retract our love because of something that was out of our control—"

"God, just stop talking!" I hollered. "All you do is talk! But what the fuck you gon' *do* about this shit, huh? I gotta bury my mothafucking sister! What the fuck are you gon' do about this!"

"Trust me, it will be handled—"

"I'm done trusting you," I told him. "Matter fact, I'm done with you, period! Now just go." I turned my back on him because I could no longer stand to look at his ass.

"Khari—"

"I think it's best if you leave, Cue," Mama finally spoke up. "We need this moment of solitude to grieve in peace."

Nodding his head in understanding, he backed off respectively. "Okay...Take as much time as you need," he said. "And when you're ready, Khari, just know I'm here for you."

29

CUE

As I left out the hospital, I contemplated how I would handle the situation at hand. My girl's sister was dead, she blamed me, and I held myself accountable for not murdering Aubrey before he had a chance to pull some shit like this.

I guess in a way Khari was right.

It was my fault.

No way in hell that nigga should still be alive after shooting Ali—but apparently I'd been slacking in my hunt to find him and kill him. But now I planned on putting that pressure on his ass.

Aubrey was a different animal.

What type of man killed their baby mama's sister in retaliation?

Our beef had nothing to do with Kylie—or Khari for that matter. His issue was with me. Kylie was simply a casualty.

Or was she?

Suddenly, it dawned on me that her death might've been an accident.

I stopped in my tracks and thought about going back to tell Khari, but I knew that she needed her space. Besides, the truth would probably only upset her more. And I didn't want to scare her or Ali.

Instead, I pulled out my phone and called up a couple Migos. The Vasquez Mexican Cartel supplied and protected me—and I knew they wouldn't let anything happen to Khari. I'd be damned if she ended up like her sister or Starr.

I would never be able to live with myself if something happened to her or my son.

30

KHARI

You're on your own, in a world you've grown...

Few more years to go...

Don't let the hurdle fall...

So be the girl you loved...

Be the girl you loved...

I'll wait, so show me why you're strong...

Ignore everybody else...

We're alone now...

Listening to James Blake's "*Retrograde*" on repeat, I flipped through the family photo album for what felt like the hundredth time. I still had trouble believing my sister was really gone. Had it not been for me making funeral arrangements, I probably would still be in denial.

It felt like I was trapped in someone else's nightmare. Khari's death just didn't seem real. It'd affected me so heavily, that I refused to look at my own reflection, because every time I did I saw her.

Suddenly I'm hip...

Is this darkness of the dawn...?

And our friends are gone...

And our friends won't come...

So show me where you fit…

Tears slid down my cheeks as the soulful lyrics filled my heart.

I had blamed Cue for Kylie's death when secretly I believed it was my own fault. If I'd been more aggressive in my attempt to refine her, I may've just saved her life. But I didn't…because the truth was, I'd given up on her.

What type of sister was I?

Suddenly, I choked back tears. I would never forgive myself for letting this happen to Kylie. I should've been there to protect her. I should've done a better job at keeping her on the right path. I should've…

My thoughts trailed off, because I knew there was nothing I could do to bring her back.

I ain't shit, I told myself.

I loved to pretend like I was this perfect, God-fearing woman who could do no wrong but deep down, I knew I wasn't shit.

I'd lied to Cue and Aubrey about Ali for years with no remorse. I had Mama thinking Aubrey was simply a record producer and not a drug dealer. I had done so much foul shit that was finally catching up with me. And I knew, in my heart, that Kylie's death was no one else's fault but my own.

I ain't shit!

I had pushed and pushed—until Aubrey finally decided to push back.

Now my sister was dead.

She was really gone—and that was on me. No one but me.

God, please forgive me for my transgressions. Pull us from the danger that's plagued this family. Please God. Watch over us, I prayed.

I could not take losing another person that I loved.

I just didn't have it in me.

31

CUE

Kylie's memorial service was held at St. James Baptist Church—the very first place she was baptized. It was a small gathering that only consisted of her closest friends and relatives.

It was my first time seeing Khari since she lashed out on me at the hospital and I wasn't quite sure how to approach her, so I kept my distance. I refused to put pressure on her during a time when it was obvious she needed her space.

If and when she was ready for me, I'd be there, no questions asked. But it was up to her to make that call. I just hoped she didn't take too long because I missed the fuck out of her and Ali.

Speaking of Ali, when he saw me, he ran up and hugged me, assuring me that his feelings for me hadn't changed. Kneeling down in front of him, I asked how he was holding up in sign language.

I'm fine...but mommy not so much, he said.

After hearing that, I looked over in Khari's direction. She didn't look very happy about my presence.

"Ali, come here," she stated. It was obvious she didn't want me talking to him.

She must've been still pretty angry with me, but I didn't mind. If blaming me helped her cope, then I would gladly be the punching bag for her emotions. Hell, I'd carry her burdens if I could. I loved her just that much, and it hurt me to know she was hurting.

After Khari and her mother spoke at the podium, I decided to share a few words of my own that touched everyone in the room—including Khari.

Kylie and I had grown up together, so her death wasn't easy on me either. She'd become a permanent fixture in my life—the little sister I never had, and it was hard for me to accept that she was gone.

After I climbed down from the podium, Mama hugged me and thanked me for speaking. I was relieved to know that she wasn't harboring any ill feelings towards me. "We're having a Passover at the house after the burial. We'd love to have you there."

When I looked over at Khari, she turned her head and folded her arms. "Thanks Ms. McKnight...but uh, I think it'd be best if I didn't. I don't wanna impose—"

"Nonsense, Cue. You're like a son to me," she said. "Khari's just going through a lot right now. Give her some time. She'll come around."

Khari must've sensed that we were talking about her because she walked over, looking like she wanted to slap me again. Before I could offer my condolences, she blurted out the last thing I expected to hear.

"I'm pregnant."

32

KHARI

SIX MONTHS LATER

Waddling through the house, I packed the last of our belongings into a moving box labeled *kitchen*. I was so ready to leave Atlanta behind that it wasn't even funny. At nearly seven months pregnant, I was anxious to start somewhere new with my family.

After taking Cue back, he proposed to me and we set a date for next year for the wedding. With the move, the pregnancy, and everything that happened, we couldn't tie the knot as soon as I'd wanted, but I didn't mind the wait.

Cue knew that I wanted our wedding to be big and lavish. And I certainly wasn't trying to walk down the aisle with this big ass belly. Because I was carrying two babies, I was damn near the size of a house—even though Cue constantly lied and told me I wasn't.

He and I were having a little boy and girl. Twins. Ironically, it seemed to run in the family.

Ali was super excited about being a big brother and I couldn't wait for him to meet his siblings. More importantly, I couldn't wait to drop this load, because carrying twins was no joke. It took a lot out of me, but I wouldn't trade the pregnancy for anything in the world.

I looked forward to a future with the man who'd helped me heal and grow after my sister's death. Cue was there for me and he supported me until I was strong enough to stand on my own two feet, and I would forever be grateful for that.

Suddenly, the front door opened and Cue walked in with food from my favorite Chinese takeout spot. I was so happy that he picked something up, because I certainly didn't have the energy to cook. I was exhausted from packing all day long. We were scheduled to move next week.

"Hey, baby."

"Hey, beautiful." Cue kissed my forehead. "How you feeling?"

"Like I'm ready to drop these babies you put in me," I laughed.

Cue chuckled. "Won't be too long. They'll be here before you know it."

I rubbed my rotund belly. "Well, I wish they would get here faster. My back's killing me."

"I told you to let me hire some help—"

"You know how I feel about strangers in my house."

Ever since Kylie's death, I didn't trust anyone coming to my home. I preferred to cook and clean myself as opposed to having a maid— even though Cue could very well afford one.

"Here. Eat something," he said, handing me

a bag of food.

"Thanks. I'm freaking starving."

"Where's my lil' man?" Cue asked.

"In his room playing that damn Wii."

A few months back, Cue and I sat Ali down and had a long-awaited talk with him. At first it was hard for him to understand that Aubrey wasn't his real father. For all of his life, he was all Ali knew, so to tell him that he wasn't biologically his son wasn't easy. But thankfully, he seemed pretty receptive to Cue being his dad, because of the bond they shared before the truth came out.

Cue took a seat beside me. "You ready for this move?"

Cue had a big, beautiful mansion built for us out in the mountains of Denver, Colorado. It featured a pool out back, a gym, a theater, a gourmet kitchen, and Italian marble throughout. It was a great place to raise a family.

I looked at him and smiled. "As ready as I'll ever be."

"You're not nervous about moving to a new state?"

I shrugged. "I'm confident in anything we do together, Cue."

Hearing me say that made him smile. "I feel the same way."

33

AUBREY

Parked outside of Khari's crib, I watched her from a distance like a mothafucking stalker. Seeing her belly grow by the day made me more and more enraged. I couldn't believe this bitch had really gotten knocked up by some other nigga. And to make matters worse, she was now playing house with the mothafucka.

Envy boiled within me after peeping the moving truck in her driveway. She planned on running off into the sunset with that nigga—but little did she know, she'd be going into the ground with him.

After her sister's accidental death, I decided to fall back for a minute in order to plot. I couldn't afford any more fuck ups, and while I wanted them dead, I didn't think I had it in me to kill Khari myself.

I mean shit. She was the love of my life for nearly ten years. I couldn't look her in the fucking face and pull the trigger...but I damn sure knew who would.

Ashing the blunt I was smoking, I pulled out my phone and called my hitta. It was time for that nigga to come out of retirement. I needed them bitches and their bastard ass babies handled once and for all.

34

TOUCHÉ

TWO DAYS LATER

Pulling on a pair of black leather driving gloves, I walked up to Khari's house, prepared to finish what I had started. After watching the place and learning Cue's routine, I decided it was best to strike during his absence. First I would kill her and the kid, and then I would murder him, slowly. That way, I touched a nerve before I put a bullet in him.

Cue deserved to feel my pain.

He wouldn't truly know what it felt like to lose someone he loved until it happened to him. I couldn't wait to exact my revenge. I blamed him and Khari for Kylie's accidental death. They might as well have been the ones who pulled the trigger.

This shit just wasn't about business—or a check. This shit was personal. I'd been itching to kill them mothafuckas, and once I got the call from Aubrey, I knew I wouldn't fuck up this time. I owed it to myself to seek vengeance.

High on coke, I approached the front door of Khari's house. The niggas Cue hired to keep watch were sitting in their cars with bullets in their skulls. It didn't matter how many watch dogs he had. They couldn't outsmart a trained assassin like me.

With a sawed off shotgun in my possession, I kicked her door open like SWAT and ran inside. Khari was on her way to the kitchen when I suddenly caught her off guard.

"ALI, GO TO YOUR ROOM AND LOCK THE DOOR!" she screamed, forgetting that her son was deaf. He wouldn't even hear me sneaking up on him until it was too late.

Khari tried to run to him but I quickly chased her and snatched her from behind by her hair.

"SOMEBODY, HELP M—"

I punched her dead in the face with a closed fist, causing her to fall on her stomach.

All of a sudden, her son appeared in the doorway. He took one look at me, the gun in my hand, and bolted off running.

I started to go after the lil' mothafucka, but Khari grabbed my pants leg in an attempt to stop me. "Leave him alone!"

WHAP!

I kicked that bitch right in her fucking face like a soccer ball. "That lil' nigga could wait," I told her. "'Cuz I'mma have some fun wit'chu first."

There was no escaping my wrath.

Turning her over onto her back, I punched her repeatedly until I felt her nose break. I'd been waiting for this shit for so long, and I wasn't going to take it easy on her. Matter fact, I was so happy about beating her that it made my dick hard.

WHAP!

WHAP!

WHAP!

WHAP!

I hit that bitch in every part of her body, including her stomach. I ain't give a fuck about her babies. I planned on beating them bitches up out of her. In my eyes, she was the reason Kylie was dead.

WHAP!

WHAP!

WHAP!

"You fucking bitch!" I yelled, foaming at the mouth. "I should've killed yo' ass a long time ago!" Wrapping my hands around her throat, I proceeded to strangle the life out of her.

"Get off my mommy!" Ali screamed, punching my back with his little fists.

"Fuck off lil' nigga! I'mma deal wit'chu later!" I shoved the shit out of his ass, but he came back swinging even harder. He was determined to protect his mother, even if it cost him his own life.

Fuck it.

Climbing off Khari, I grabbed my shotgun and pointed it at him.

"NO!"

Khari jumped on my back and bit the side of my neck, snatching out a chunk of muscle. "*Ahhh*, shit!"

I flipped her ass over and slammed her onto the floor.

Ali quickly took off running in fear.

I started to go after him, but I figured it was better to take care of Khari first. "Leave him alone! He's just a kid! He has nothing to do with this," she said with a mouthful of blood. Her teeth were painted dark red and her face was swollen to the point of being unrecognizable. I'd really fucked her ass up but it just didn't feel like it was enough for me.

WHAM!

I kicked her in the face, knocking out several teeth.

"Fuck that lil' nigga and fuck you, bitch."

Climbing on top of her, I pinned her down and ripped off her shirt.

"That lil' bitch can watch me fuck you before I put a bullet in his head!"

When I reached for her pants, I felt something warm and wet between her legs. I quickly realized that it was blood—but I didn't give a fuck. It damn sure wouldn't stop me from ripping her open.

"Get the fuck off me!" she cried.

I smiled and reached for my belt. "The more you struggle, the more I'll enjoy it."

I was just about to pull my dick out when I felt something hard and heavy crash down onto my skull. Before I knew what the fuck happened, everything suddenly went black.

35
CUE

My Migo was about to put a bullet in Touché's head after knocking him out, but I quickly stopped him. "No!"

"*El se lo merece*," he argued, expressing that Touché deserved it.

"No. Keep his ass alive." I had something in store for that sick, twisted mothafucka. "Go get my boy. Make sure he's okay."

"*Si jefe.*"

Luckily, I got back when I did, or else he would've had his way. When I looked down at my fiancé, I saw that she was bleeding badly and battling consciousness. Gently scooping her into my arms, I carried her outside to the car.

"Don't worry. I got'chu, bay. Everything's gonna be okay." A tear slipped from my eye and rolled down my cheek. I almost couldn't bare seeing her in this condition. But I knew I had to be strong for both of us—and for our unborn children."

"No it isn't," she cried. "The...babies..." She struggled to touch her stomach. "Something's wrong...I can feel it! Something's wrong with my babies!"

***

After rushing Khari to the hospital, she was given an emergency C-section. The twins survived despite the abuse and being born two months premature. They were less than a pound when doctors pulled them Khari's from womb and no bigger than the size of my hand.

At only 1 pound and 11 oz., they were far too fragile and tiny to breathe on their own. They could barely even open their eyes.

The first 48 hours after their birth was extremely nerve-wracking. And every single minute of the day, I prayed for God to help them fight to survive. I didn't know what the fuck I'd do if I lost them.

With Ali being deaf, I didn't quite know what to expect. And if they did have any disabilities, I didn't care, as long as they were alive and healthy.

The doctors were painstaking honest when it came to our expectations. They were unsure if the babies would survive, but they assured us they would do everything in their power to make sure they did.

Every day I sat by their incubator, waiting for them to pull through. And while I looked after them, Ali looked after his mom. Khari had suffered two fractured ribs and a broken nose, but thankfully the injuries were not life-threatening. If I hadn't come back, there was no telling what all Touché would've done to her and my son.

Speaking of Touché, I planned on torturing that mothafucka until he begged me to put him out of his misery. He had to pay for this shit—and so did Aubrey.

36

KHARI

I couldn't believe that I had to wait an entire week before I was able to hold my babies for the first time. They were so small, so fragile, and yet they were fighters. Even with all of the abuse I'd sustained, they were born with no health issues.

Doctors informed us that they'd have to spend the first few months of their life in the hospital, but they would be healthy normal babies. I couldn't have been any happier—especially considering the circumstances.

Mommy, can I hold them, Ali asked in sign language.

"They're far too tiny now, baby. But once they get bigger and stronger, I promise you can hold them whenever you want for as long as you want."

"Okay," he beamed, excited to finally be a big brother.

Cue sat silently at my side as he admired the twins. We had named them Khaison and Kylie—after my sister of course. If she was here, I knew she would've been proud. They were my miracle babies.

"They're strong...just like their mother," Cue said.

I became emotional when I thought about them being put in harm's way.

"Ali, do me a favor and get mommy a glass of water, please."

"Okay!" He quickly jumped up, anxious to wait on me hand and foot. He'd been quite the support system throughout my hospital stay and I was so blessed to have him.

After Ali walked off, I turned towards Cue. I didn't want our son to read my lips and judge me for what I was about to say.

"Cue, we have to kill him."

He reached over and caressed my shoulder. "He'll be dealt with accordingly."

I started crying after realizing I sounded like a monster. "I'm sorry. It's just...I can't stand the thought of something happening to them—"

"You and the kids are everything to me, Khari. And I will do whatever it takes to protect you all. Don't worry," I told her. "I'm not letting Aubrey touch me, my money, or my family. I will handle it. Trust and believe."

37
CUE

"Wake the fuck up, pussy nigga!" I tossed a bucket-full of scalding hot water on Touché after walking in and finding him unconscious. He was tied to a chair in an abandoned warehouse, and missing several fingers.

I planned on torturing him slowly over time. First, I would take all of his fingers, and then his limbs. And if that didn't kill him, I would begin to remove his organs one by one. It was sick, but it was a punishment that was fitting for a sick mothafucka like him.

Touché cried and howled in pain as his skin sizzled and blistered with puss.

"I told you I'd be back. I don't know why the fuck you fell asleep."

I was too upbeat about killing this mothafucka slowly. In my opinion, he wasn't getting shit he didn't deserve. He'd almost taken my family from me. Now it was my turn to take shit from him—piece by mothafucking piece.

Touché started panicking as soon as he saw me walk over towards the table of the torture instruments. I had all types of shit laid out. Hammers, pliers, a razor sharp knife, a steel bat wrapped in barbed wire, a machete, and a heavy, rusted crowbar.

"C'mon, man, please...I can't take no more of this shit. Just kill me," he begged.

I didn't look at him when I answered, "That'll take all the fun out of it."

"Please," Touché cried. "You got the wrong nigga, man. Aubrey paid me to do that shit. I ain't wanna do it, man. You gotta believe me!"

I grabbed the razor sharp knife. "You're gonna die," I told him. "That's no negotiating. At least try to die with a lil' dignity."

Touché started rocking in his seat. "*Pleeeeeeeaaasssseeeee!*"

"Hold still," I said. "I need to take a few more of those fingers."

I was about to cut his index finger off when he said, "I have money! I can pay you whatever the fuck you want, man! Just let me go!"

I laughed at weak and pathetic he looked. He'd quickly gone from bold to bitch in a matter of days—and I was just getting started.

"You keep that money, my dude. Ya folks can use it to pay for a nice funeral...Or a cremation. Hell, after all, there won't be much left of you when I'm down. I doubt they'll want an open casket."

Touché began freaking out after hearing that.

I wanted to torture him physically and

psychologically.

"I—I can give you Aubrey!" he desperately said. "I know where you can find the nigga! I can tell you where he's at! I'll give him to you, man. Just please let me go!"

There was a long, tension-filled silence between us.

Touché pleaded with his eyes for me to reason. He would sell his soul if that meant freedom. He damn sure didn't mind giving up Aubrey.

Suddenly, I grabbed him by throat. "I already know. But thanks anyway," I said before carving out his left eye.

The bloodcurdling screams that came after was music to my ears.

38

CUE

Khari didn't know it, but after the birth of the twins, I had Aubrey's bandos torched and safe houses hit. The niggas that worked the corners for him were brutally killed by men—along with anyone else in association. I even had his niggas in prison murdered and anybody repping that GD shit.

I was on some straight homicidal shit.

I ain't play about my family and now everyone in Atlanta would know it

I had a 2-million-dollar bounty on Aubrey's head that ran him out the city. Little did he know, there was nowhere he could run or hide. There was no escaping me or what I had planned for him.

Because I had a network of informants working for me, it didn't take long to find out he was holed up in a motel out in Savannah. He should've fled the country, but the stupid mothafucka ain't even have enough sense to flee the state.

That mistake would cost him dearly.

***

Three hours later, I arrived at the flea pit motel Aubrey temporarily called home. When I saw his whip parked out front, I knew he was inside. After slipping the concierge a few thousands, I quickly found which room he was located in.

Wielding the rusty crowbar, I chose to roll solo for this occasion.

I could've had my killers handle his ass, but for everything he'd done, I wanted to be the one to put him down. I planned on killing that mothafucka with my bare hands.

Fuck a gun.

All I needed was a sturdy and a vest.

When I reached his door, I kicked that bitch off the hinges—and nearly vomited by what I saw.

Aubrey was getting his dick sucked by a young boy that looked no older than sixteen or seventeen. I knew Aubrey was fucked in the head, but I had no idea he was a sick, twisted, deviant pervert.

Aubrey took one look at me and quickly reached for his strap on the nightstand—

I threw the crowbar at him before he could grab it, hitting him right in the forehead with it.

The young boy ran past me naked and out of the room.

I was glad that he didn't stick around for what I had planned.

Blood gushed from the gaping wound on Aubrey's head, and he was left dazed and confused. Grabbing his gun, I tucked it in my waist.

For the first time in his life, he was alone and vulnerable. I had isolated him, making it that much easier for me to corner him.

"All of this could've been avoided had you just stayed yo' ass in prison," I told him.

"Fuck you!" he spat.

I laughed at his brazenness. He knew he was about to die, and yet he still wanted to play the tough guy role. "Nah, you fucked yaself."

CLUNK!

I cracked his ass in the head with the crowbar, busting his shit wide open.

Aubrey fell off the bed, onto the floor—where I proceeded to beat him unmercifully.

"This is for Kylie."

CLUNK!

"This is for Khari."

CLUNK!

"This is for my babies!"

CLUNK!

"This is for me!"

CLUNK!

I beat the shit out of Aubrey until his skull caved in and his face was unrecognizable.

His eyeball socket was exposed after the sixth time I struck him. When I hit him again, it completely flew out his head.

CLUNK!

CLUNK!

CLUNK!

I continued to beat him until I was literally dripping with sweat and he was nothing more than a neck and a body. By the time I exhausted myself, there was nothing left of his face but a lower jaw and a few teeth.

Grabbing the gun off my waist, I emptied the clip into his body for the fuck of it. I made sure Aubrey's death was brutal and horrific, but in the end, it still felt like it was too good for a mothafucka like him. Walking out of the room, I left Aubrey in a puddle of his own blood, bones, and guts.

Good fucking riddance.

EPILOGUE

KHARI

ONE YEAR LATER

"Dearly Beloved, we are gathered together here to join together this man and this woman in holy matrimony, which is commended to be honorable among all men—and therefore, to not be entered into unadvisedly or lightly, but reverently, discreetly, advisedly and solemnly."

Cue and I gazed into each other's eyes as we were sworn into marriage by God. We had a small wedding ceremony out in Dubai, where only our closest relatives and friends were invited. Both our mothers were among the attendees. It would've been nice if Kylie was as well, but I knew she was watching over me from heaven.

"Through marriage, Cue and Khari make a commitment together to face their disappointments, embrace their dreams, realize their hopes, and accept each other's failures."

I looked over at our children and smiled. They were all in the front row, watching intently. Thankfully, the twins had made a full recovery and were healthier than the average. Cue was right. They were strong. Just like their parents.

"We are here today before God because marriage is one of His most sacred wishes to witness the joining in marriage of Cue and Khari.

This occasion marks the celebration of love and commitment with which this man and this woman begin their life together. And now, through me, He joins you together in one of the holiest bonds."

Cue took my hands in his once it was time to exchange vows. "Khari, you've made me the happiest man alive today," he smiled. "I promise to love you for you and to trust what I do not yet know. You never have to worry about catering to my preferences. Because since I've met you, all my preferences were reset. You're perfect for me, Khari. And I vow to respect you as an individual, a partner, and as an equal. I promise to laugh with you when times are good, and endure with you when they are bad. I will always adore, honor and encourage you. You are my best friend, and I will love you forever."

His touching words brought tears to my eyes. Swallowing my anxieties, I prepared to recite my vows. "I promise to love and care for you, and I will try in every way, to be worthy of your love. I will always be honest with you, kind, patient and forgiving. But most of all, I promise to be a true and loyal friend to you. I love you, Cue...I don't know what more to say than that."

He teared up and smiled after I read my vows. "There's nothing more needed, baby."

"Do you Cue take Khari to be your wife, to live together after God's ordinance, in the holy estate of matrimony? Will you love her, comfort her, honor and keep her, in sickness and in health, for richer, for poorer, for better, for worse, in sadness and in joy, to cherish and continually bestow upon her your heart's deepest devotion, forsaking all others, keep yourself only unto her as long as you both shall live?"

"I will," Cue said.

"Do you Khari take Cue to be your husband, to live together after God's ordinance, in the holy estate of matrimony? Will you love him, comfort him, honor and keep him, in sickness and in health, for richer, for poorer, for better, for worse, in sadness and in joy, to cherish and continually bestow upon him your heart's deepest devotion, forsaking all others, keep yourself only unto him as long as you both shall live?"

"I will."

Cue and I exchanged wedding rings.

"May these rings be blessed as the symbol of this affectionate unity. These two lives are now joined in one unbroken circle. Wherever they go, may they always return to one another. May these two find in each other the love for which all men and women yearn. May they grow in understanding and in compassion. I now pronounce you husband and wife."

When he grabbed and kissed me, I knew right then that everything would be okay.

THE END

1

"See, this is why I fuck with this place. The water's nice and hot, and the service is consistent. Not like that bullshit you took us to over there on Piedmont a few weeks back," Monica laughed.

Monica and Femi dipped their toes inside the pedicure bowl simultaneously. Every two weeks they met for either fill-ins or pedicures while catching each other up on the latest drama. Last week, Femi wanted to try somewhere new, but the service stunk and Monica wouldn't let her friend live that shit down.

Now in their early thirties, both women had been friends since freshman year in high school. Monica, who was slightly chubby, was a beautiful woman with coffee brown skin and a cherubic face. She looked a lot like television personality, Shekinah, and always wore her hair in an asymmetrical bob. She made a decent wage working full-time as a local celebrity stylist.

Femi, born to West Indian parents, was dark brown with wide, bright eyes, full lips, and a curvy figure. At 5'9, she was taller than average, and most people often told her she resembled Keisha from the movie *Belly*.

"If you want chair massage, the remote next to you," the Vietnamese nail technician said in broken English.

"Thank you," Femi smiled. Relaxing in the seat, she hit the button, and allowed the chair to kneed away her stress and tension. No more than two minutes later, her phone rang. The call was from an unrecognizable number, so she hesitated on answering it.

"What's up?" Monica asked, noticing something was wrong.

Femi sighed and ran a hand through her natural, long hair. Her husband never wanted her to wear weave, because he thought she looked better without it. She loved her sew-ins but she would do just about anything to keep him happy.

"Another unknown calling me," Femi said. "You know what the fuck that means."

Monica snorted and shook her head in disgust. "I don't see how you put up with it, Femi. That nigga got all these hoes calling you like he ain't got a whole fucking wife at home. The shit pisses me off and he ain't even my man."

"I'm just not gonna answer it." Femi placed her phone down on the small table next to her chair. It stopped ringing for a short period, but started again after a few seconds. When it was obvious that she wouldn't pick up, a series of text messages poured in.

"Bitch, you a good one. I would've divorced that dirty dick dog years ago—"

"Monica!" Femi lashed out. She was embarrassed that customers and employees were in earshot. She also didn't need to be reminded about the STDs.

"I'm sorry, but it's true. I don't see how the fuck you deal. Are you his main or his mistress, 'cuz I don't fucking get it—"

"And you won't," Femi cut in. "He's *my* husband, Monica. You wouldn't understand. When was the last time you had a man, '06?"

"2005 to be exact," Monica corrected her. "And that's why...'cuz niggas ain't shit. You give them one hundred and muthafuckas can't even give fifty percent."

Femi's cellphone continued to ring, only adding to her list of frustrations. Unable to ignore the constant calls, she finally answered in a snappy tone. "What?!"

A sultry but raspy female's voice filled the speaker. "Did you get my pictures?" Trina asked. The sarcasm in her tone made Femi want to reach through the phone and slap her.

"Which one is it this time?" Monica asked in the background. She'd grown equally used to the phone calls from multiple women.

Sucking her teeth, Femi pulled the phone away from her face and looked at the texts. Her blood boiled after seeing a plethora of photos with Trina and her husband looking real cozy. In every picture he was either sleeping or caught off guard completely. The bitch had to sneak a pic just to capture a photo of him. It was pathetic.

"You're interrupting my foot scrub, hoe," Femi stated. Her husband hadn't been home in two weeks. Due to business he traveled a lot, so there was never no telling what the nigga was up to. "What the fuck do you want?" she asked, cutting to the chase. Femi put Trina on speaker, so that her girl could hear how ridiculous she sounded.

"I thought the pictures were pretty self-explanatory," Trina laughed. She wanted Femi's husband. That much was obvious.

"Hand me the phone. I'll tell the hoe off," Monica said with her palm outstretched. "Either give it here, or hang up on that bih."

Trina heard Monica in the distance. Desperate to get a reaction before Femi hung up, she said, "Did you know he got me pregnant a few months back?"

Femi's entire face grew hot. It felt as if her heart had dropped to the pit of her stomach. The entire nail salon had heard the bomb she dropped. If Trina were anywhere within arm's reach, Femi would've strangled her. Jumping out of the chair with soaking wet feet, she ran outside so no one would hear her tirade. "What the fuck did you just say?!"

Her man had the young hoes going crazy. Upset about the empty promises made to them, they had nothing better to do than to call and torment Femi. It seemed like every other month she went through the same shit, but he never changed, and she never left.

"You heard me. I ain't stutter! Yo' nigga got me pregnant. Wasn't too hard since he be nutting in this pussy every week." Trina laughed wickedly. She could tell by Femi's silence that she'd gotten to her. "Looks like our kids gon' be siblings."

"Over my dead body," Femi told her.

"It's already done, boo. Don't feel so fucking good, does it? Knowing that nigga knocked me up after making you burn your tubes. You must feel pretty fucking stupid—"

Trina's sentence was cut short after Monica grabbed the phone and hung up. She'd run outside to make sure her girl was okay. She had never seen Femi snap like that. Usually, she didn't let hoes get her out of her hookup, but today Trina had pushed her buttons.

"Fuck that bitch," Monica said. "She's probably lying just to get a rise out of you. Don't give that silly hoe the satisfaction."

"You know my husband just as well as I do. I doubt that bitch is lying, M. And whether she is or ain't, he had no right telling these hoes our fucking business!" Femi was livid that he would do something like that. What the hell was he thinking? He knew how she felt about getting her tubes tied. She'd only done it because he made her. Now she was being told that he'd gotten some random bitch pregnant behind her back. Femi was so hurt that she couldn't hold back the tears. "I'm gonna kill that dirty mothafucka!"

2

    Seventeen-year old Kirby Caldwell multi-tasked between carrying a tray of food and drinks to the table of fine ass men straight ahead. Judging from their swagger and poise, they didn't look like they were from Philly. Couldn't be. The European designer clothing, shiny jewelry, and expensive cologne screamed foreign. Kirby was drawn to them instantly like moths to a flame. The boys she saw on an everyday basis were certainly not of their caliber.

    These niggas are the real deal. Ever since they walked in, Kirby had been wracking her brain about what they did for a living. They were far from being the blue-collar type. They had trouble written all over, but for some reason she was still drawn to them.

    Maybe they're staying upstairs in the Windsor suites, Kirby thought to herself. The customers at the pub she worked at were mainly guests who took advantage of the discount offered by the hotel.

    As soon as Kirby reached their table, she pushed her thoughts to the back of her mind. All four men were in deep in conversation prior to her arrival but stopped the minute she approached them.

    Kirby felt odd as each man sized her up. It made her nervous, because she knew they were trying to decide if they appreciated what they saw. She was thin with A-cup breasts, small hips, and an ass she thought was too big for her tiny frame. In her opinion Kirby thought she was just average. Nothing special, but nothing too bad to look at. One of her admirers, on the other hand, held an entirely different sentiment.

"Aye, you got a tough lil' body on you, ma. That thing pokin' too. How old is you, if you don't mind me askin'?" Aviance's eyes traveled the length of Kirby's petite body. He loved a skinny bitch with a fat ass. Someone he could easily manhandle while sticking the pipe to.

At only 20, he was the most flamboyant of the quartet. They were only politicking over dinner, and the nigga had on two diamond chains and a sparkling diamond grill. If it weren't for the fact that he kept a shooter 'round him, he would've been robbed countless times.

Aviance was damn near blinding everyone in the establishment, but he loved showing off. He also loved gorgeous women, and never bit his tongue when it came to expressing it. A smirk pulled at his full lips as he admired what he saw. Kirby was definitely his type. He was just about to go in for the kill when his boss cut in.

"Ease up, bruh. Swear yo' ass don't know how to act whenever you see a bad bitch. My bad, you gotta excuse my nephew."

After hearing the word 'bitch', Kirby did an automatic double take. She started to check his ass when suddenly she noticed how fine he was. She damn near spilled the drinks looking.

Smooth midnight black skin, pearl white teeth, chiseled jawline, and muscular build. *Gotdamn.* He looked like an African king—like the tribal warriors she read about in her black History books. He was beautiful.

Castle looked every bit of the boss he was in a black Givenchy tee and black high top Giuseppes. A black and gray Louis Vuitton belt secured his tan designer jeans. He had $120,000 on his wrist like money grew on trees.

I bet his ass got a flock of hoes at his beck and call though, Kirby presumed. Although she told herself that, she tampered with the thought of possibly being one of them. It must've been nice. She then laughed inside after realizing how out of her league he was. There he sat, draped in expensive clothes and jewelry while she waited on tables.

Kirby imagined him only dating Beyonces and Rihannas anyway. *I got as much chance ending up with him as I do hitting the lottery*, she told herself. *Keep dreaming.*

Nervously clearing her throat, Kirby placed the dishes in their respectable places and rushed off before she embarrassed herself. Her best friend, McKenzie was patiently awaiting her arrival behind the bar. She, too, was a waitress at the pub they worked at. The quaint mom and pop restaurant didn't get much business other than that of hotel guests, so they stood around talking shit all day until it was time to clock out.

"Girl, I'm so fucking jealous. I was praying I got their section," McKenzie joked. "Them jawns fine as shit, ain't they. And that dark-skinned one could get the mothafucking business. I'm just saying." She had a weakness for chocolate men.

Although Kirby and McKenzie were like sisters, they were as different as night and day. At 18, McKenzie was a tall, slender redbone with mint green eyes, freckles, and reddish brown hair that she inherited from her white daddy. He had walked out on her when she was just two-years old. This was after his wife found out about his sidepiece. McKenzie was a product of messiness. She was also very promiscuous.

Sometimes Kirby wondered if she was that way because of what her father did. Kirby reserved her judgment since they were girls despite her mother's constant warnings about the company she kept. She had never really cared for McKenzie.

"I'm not gonna lie, they low-key had me nervous. I wish you had gotten their section too. I dread having to go back over there," Kirby laughed.

"Damn, Kirbz, you gotta stop acting so scared of niggas. I swear, every time you get in the presence of a dude you retreat—"

"Bullshit," Kirby argued.

"Bitch, you practically ran from that section," McKenzie reminded her. "Besides, name the last time you even dealt with a nigga...and kindergarten don't count—"

"Don't come for me, sweetie. I told you I dry pumped in the girl's bathroom once and you won't let that shit go," Kirby laughed.

"Bitch, that was your best and *only* experience," her friend teased. "You need to get you some real dick, and quit acting so timid." McKenzie often teased her friend about her virgin status.

"Don't try to come down on me just 'cuz my track record don't match yours. When I'm ready I will."

Instead of entertaining Kirby's low blow, McKenzie pointed back to the fellas' table. "*Ooh, look.* One of 'em still checking you out," she giggled. "That mothafucka is too damn fine. What'd you do to that man, bish?"

Kirby was almost scared to crane her neck. "Girl, quit playing. I haven't done anything." When she finally turned to look she noticed Castle staring directly at her. Kirby didn't know it yet, but he had already staked his claim on the young woman.

***

Since Kirby's shift ended three hours before McKenzie's she wound up catching the bus alone. Once she was let off at her stop, she walked the rest of the way. The routine had become as normal as breathing. South Philly wasn't exactly a safe haven, but she'd been living there all her life.

Kirby often dreamt about the day she was able to move out the hood and buy her first whip. She already knew what she wanted: a pearl white Mercedes Benz with shiny chrome rims. Instead of saving up for her dream car, Kirby had to pay utility and hospital bills. Three years ago her mom, Leah lost her left breast to cancer. It went in remission for a little while, but was now back and more aggressive than ever. Leah's heaping medical expenses left them bankrupt. The government assistance helped out some, but it wasn't nearly enough to support a dying woman and her teenage children.

Kirby's brother, Kaleb was a year older than her and stayed in and out of jail. He'd done everything from robbing to stealing in order to provide for his family—but the law eventually caught up with him.

It had been two years since the police kicked her door off the hinges to apprehend him. They dragged Kaleb off faster than they were able to read his Miranda rights. He was only seventeen at the time. They charged him for stealing and flipping cars, and he was left to rot in a human zoo.

In the beginning, Kaleb used to write his sister religiously, but over time his communication eventually slowed down. She figured he might've just wanted to serve his time in solitude. Though Kirby missed him, she wouldn't dare become a burden. She didn't know what he was going through alone in prison, but she didn't want to add more to his plate with her troubles. Kirby figured the least she could do was take care of mom and hold things down until he was released—whenever that was.

All of a sudden, the light blaring of a horn interrupted Kirby's thoughts. She noticed a shiny black Rolls Royce ease alongside her. The driver of the fancy vehicle made sure to match his pace with her walking.

"Aye, why you out here walkin' alone, mama. You need a ride or somethin'?"

Kirby recognized the voice before she did the driver. Seeing him again, and so unexpectedly, made her nervous. He made her palms sweat and her stomach flip-flop. *Damn*. What was it about him that made her get butterflies and fall apart whenever she was in his presence? What the hell was he doing in her hood anyway?

Kirby looked around to make sure he wasn't talking to someone else. It seemed almost impossible for him to show an interest in her. Someone who was flat-chested and average at best. She wondered if he was fucking with her for the hell of it. It would've been a crude thing to do if he was.

Just keep walking.

Kirby told herself one thing, but her curiosity outweighed her common sense.

"Aye, don't act like you don't see me." The hint of humor in his tone was enough to let her know he wasn't too serious. "I ain't from 'round here but I know it ain't safe for a young lady to be walkin' alone. C'mon. I ain't gon' bite." Castle brought his car to a slow stop, reached over and opened the passenger door.

He was in Philly for business purposes, but on that side of town to visit one of his freaks—a badass stripper he'd met at *Onyx*. He was on his way to her crib when he saw something more promising from the corner of his eye. Nothing intrigued him more than the prospect of new pussy, so he did what any self-righteous nigga would. He pulled up on her ass.

Ironically, before he left the restaurant with his boys, Castle passed his number to McKenzie to give to Kirby who was in the restroom at the time. What he didn't know was that McKenzie had jealously ripped it up and tossed it out. On the low, she was mad he hadn't hollered at her first. She'd been checking for him too; she peeped Castle the minute he walked in, but it was obvious whom he was more interested in. Naturally, McKenzie wasn't feeling that shit. In her world, no man would choose Kirby over her. McKenzie believed cute light-skinned girls reigned supreme.

Unfortunately, she had no control over fate and pure coincidence. Somehow Castle and Kirby still ended up bumping into each other.

Kirby cautiously peered inside his ride to verify he was by himself. *I probably shouldn't,* she told herself. She had never actually climbed in the car with a total stranger before. Since a young girl she knew better than to ever do something so stupid. Kirby knew what she should've done. She should have continued walking...but her legs had a mind of their own as they slowly approached his flashy car.

"Is it...safe?" Kirby asked shyly. Castle made her unashamedly bashful, and he knew it was because he intimidated her. Men of his caliber didn't speak to chicks like her. Hell, they barely even gave them a second look. Castle found her nervous demeanor cute.

Chuckling at her innocent question, he asked, "How old are you, baby girl?"

"...Seventeen."

Castle refused to tell her that he had a daughter a year younger than her. "Aye, look. You in good hands, lil' mama. I promise."

Kirby slowly climbed inside, sealing her fate as soon as she closed the door. She figured there was no harm in allowing him to take her home. Besides, it wasn't like she didn't find him attractive.

"Why's it so fuckin' dark in this city? Like damn. Tax money won't cover the cost of some streetlights 'round dis mufucka? Gotta feel like you walkin' through the 'hood blind folded or some shit. You be walkin' every day at this time?"

"Yeah, but usually I'm with my girl McKenzie. We work together and she stays a block from me."

"Oh, nah. You too damn pretty to be on foot," he said, shaking his head. "If you was my bitch, I wouldn't have yo' ass walkin'."

Wale's new album played softly through his custom speakers. His interior smelled of Clive Christian cologne and top quality loud. Kirby didn't smoke, but she was familiar with the scent because Kaleb once sold it. That boy had damn near done everything under the sun just to put food in the fridge. He'd sacrificed his freedom to take care of her and their mom.

"What's yo' address?" Castle asked.

Kirby rattled off where she lived before fastening her seatbelt. She shouldn't have been so comfortable with him, but for some reason she felt like she could trust him.

After plugging her address in his GPS, he retrieved the L tucked behind his ear. He'd dropped several stacks to have a police monitor installed so that he could track how close a squad car was. Twelve loved to fuck with a nigga with some paper.

"You chief?" Castle asked, holding up the blunt.

"No," she murmured.

"You a good girl, huh?"

Kirby shrugged. "I guess so."

"Shit, they say good girls are just bad girls that never got caught..." Castle passed the blunt to Kirby again in hopes that she would hit it. He hated a square bitch.

Surprisingly, Kirby grabbed it and took a light pull. A flurry of hoarse coughs came soon after. She felt like she'd hacked up an organ. She had never smoked a day in her life. Wheezing and hacking, Kirby quickly passed the L back to Castle.

He took a couple tokes before lowering his window. "You good?"

"Yes," Kirby struggled to say.

"So what's ya name, Virgin Lungs?"

She laughed a little. "Kirby. And yours?"

"Castle Maurice Black III."

Kirby loved how regal his name sounded. It fit him so well. "Is that your real name?" she asked.

Castle laughed and it warmed her heart. She noticed that he now had a gold bottom grill in. The single piece of jewelry alone cost more than her home was worth. "Baby girl, I'm too old for aliases and nicknames, and shit."

"What's too old?" Kirby asked curiously.

"A whole lot older than you, youngin'."

"How old?" she pressed.

"Guess."

"*Hmm.*" Kirby rested an index finger on her right cheek's dimple. "I'mma say... Thirty maybe...."

Castle nodded his head appreciatively. Her irrepressible innocence and naivety captivated him. She was young enough to be molded and groomed. That was the main reason he loved young hoes. "Close," he said. "Thirty-six."

"Oh."

Castle didn't miss the flatness in her tone. "What'chu mean 'oh'?" he chuckled. "That too old for you?"

Kirby paused. Castle made her nervous. She barely knew anything about him, but she was sure she'd never met anyone like him. There was an enigmatic aura that surrounded him; he had a boss-like presence. She envisioned him as a man in charge, but she had no idea to what extent. She might've fled if she knew he was top dog of a multi-million dollar drug operation.

"I'm not sure. I never dated anyone in their thirties."

"Do you date at all," was Castle's next question.

"...Not really," Kirby answered, slightly embarrassed. She thought about lying but it was what it was. The boys at her school weren't really checking for her, and the few who did were never taken seriously. Either that, or they just weren't her type.

"So you mean to tell me yo' ass never had a boyfriend before?" he asked. "You ain't gotta lie to me, baby girl. One thing about me, I hate a fuckin' liar—"

"I'm not lying," she promised.

"You ever fucked before?"

Kirby's cheeks flushed in embarrassment. She wasn't expecting such a bold question. "No," she squeaked out.

"You ain't ever fucked before. You ain't ever had a boyfriend before. Why do I find that shit so hard to believe? How come you never had a boyfriend?"

Kirby shrugged. "I don't know. No one's really grabbed my interest, I guess."

"That's 'cuz you ain't ever fucked with a real nigga."

Castle slowly eased his car in front of Kirby's house. The building he pulled in front of hardly looked livable, but it was the destination his navigational system had led him to.

Kirby took her time unfastening her seatbelt. "Where you from, if you don't mind me asking. You mentioned you weren't from around here...and you have an accent."

"Oh yeah?" Castle chuckled, and his grill sparkled. "I'm from Atlanta, baby. Born and raised."

"That's cool. I hear a lot about Atlanta. What's it like?"

"Like Black Hollywood."

It sounded like somewhere she'd like to one-day visit. Lingering on the doorknob, Kirby almost didn't want to leave, but she knew her mother was waiting on her. As her health gradually degenerated, she had become increasingly immobile. Kirby couldn't leave her alone for extended periods.

"Shit, take my number though," he told her. "I'm only in town for a couple days, then I'm headed to Vegas. You ever been?"

"I never even left Philadelphia."

"Real shit? Damn. That's all bad. Fuck with me then. We could fly out together. It's fight weekend so shit's gon' be crazy."

"Fight weekend? What's that?"

Castle looked over at Kirby in disbelief. "You don't get out much, do you? Just a small city girl that ain't 'een stepped foot in the real world."

Kirby shrugged. She didn't have a comeback.

"Floyd and Pacquiao fightin' at the MGM."

"Who are they?"

Castle chuckled. "Boxers. Damn, baby. You live under a rock? You must not be into social media."

"Not really. Between work and school I barely have time to keep up with entertainment."

Castle loved that she wasn't big on social media. "I dig that. And ain't nothin' to be sorry about," he said. "You handlin' ya business. I like that shit. I can respect it. But yeah, like I was sayin', it's gon' be dope. I'm tryin' to brush shoulders with stars. You should fuck with a nigga. I'd show you a good time." He tried to gauge her interest with talk of celebrities.

"I can't just up and leave. I have to take care of my mama. She can't stay alone for long periods of time."

"Why? What's wrong with her?"

"She's...sick." Kirby wasn't ready to tell him that Leah was dying of cancer.

"Lemme handle that fuh you then," he offered.

"How?"

Castle shrugged like it was no big deal. "Shit, I'll pay somebody to do that."

Kirby laughed as if he'd said a joke. When she realized he was dead serious, she stopped and stared at him. She then thought about the crisp hundred-dollar tip he'd left her at the pub. "You really are for real, ain't you?"

"Do I look like a nigga that play games?" Castle took her hand in his, gently caressing her knuckles. His hands were large, rough and calloused in comparison to her smaller, softer ones. Years of prison, slinging, and gun toting had hardened him.

"No. But what about school?" Kirby asked. "I still have a couple weeks left 'til graduation—"

"Couple weeks?" he scoffed. "That's it? Well, shit, I guess we'll get up next time then. Gon' 'head and finish up ya'll lil' school year. There may be other opportunities."

Kirby didn't like the way that sounded. Castle made it seem as if she might not see him again after that day, and she wasn't feeling that.

"What if I *did* wanna go though," Kirby suddenly said. "We barely know each other...shouldn't we get to know each other first? I mean I never did this before..."

Castle could see that she was toying with the idea. Young and naïve, she couldn't help being gullible. Kirby was pure like raw cocaine—and just as lethal. Castle knew the consequences for fucking with an underage girl, but he still wanted her.

She had one of two choices. She could take the blue pill and return to her boring, everyday life while struggling to make ends meet. Or...she could take the red pill and allow Castle to make a woman out of her young ass.

"We can get to know each other on this lil' trip." Castle reached over and trailed his fingertip along her thigh. He had a solution for every excuse she hit him with. Kirby had actually run out of them altogether.

"I...I still don't know," she hesitated. "I...Maybe I need time to think about it."

"I'm leaving Thursday. So don't take too long to think about it, aight."

"I won't..." Kirby could feel things heating up between them. She'd never felt so much intensity with a guy before. "I'll call you," she said, opening the passenger door

"I'll be waitin'," he smiled. Castle enjoyed a good cat-and-mouse game, just as long as the other person made it worthwhile. He could smell that tight, illicitly sweet pussy from his seat. There was no pussy better than virgin pussy.

She bullshitting right now, but she'll be mine in no time, Castle told himself. He'd make sure of that.

Kirby carefully climbed out and headed towards her house. As she ascended the cracked stone steps, she could feel Castle's dark eyes penetrating her. If she could've saw into the future, she would've ran without looking back. She would've never climbed in his shiny Rolls

Royce...and she certainly wouldn't have called him.

It was an inauspicious beginning to a long and complex relationship.

VISIT AMAZON.COM TO GET YOUR FREE COPY OF YOUR SPOUSE, MY SPONSOR!